jock a.   .amis

Jock and Aramis

Ewan Battersby
&
Dianne Speter

An Omnibus Book from Scholastic Australia

LEXILE™ 1030

Omnibus Books
335 Unley Road, Malvern SA 5061
an imprint of Scholastic Australia Pty Ltd (ABN 11 000 614 577)
PO Box 579, Gosford NSW 2250.
www.scholastic.com.au

Part of the Scholastic Group
Sydney • Auckland • New York • Toronto • London • Mexico City •
New Delhi • Hong Kong • Buenos Aires • Puerto Rico

First published in 2005.
Text copyright © Ewan Battersby and Dianne Speter, 2005.
Map copyright © Dianne Speter and Ewan Battersby, 2005.
Cover design copyright © Omnibus Books, 2005.
Cover illustrations © David Cornish, 2005

National Library of Australia Cataloguing-in-Publication entry
Battersby, Ewan.
Jock and Aramis.
For older readers aged 12+.
ISBN 1 86291 634 9.
1. Quests (Expeditions)—Juvenile fiction. I. Speter,
Dianne. II. Title.
A823.4

Typeset in 12/18 pt Granjon by Bookhouse, Sydney.
Printed and bound by McPherson's Printing Group, Victoria.

10 9 8 7 6 5 4 3 2 1   5 6 7 8 9 / 0

For my parents — EB

To my parents,
long-time friends of Jock — DS

The continent of Annistrelle

astes of Mere

ntains

zarelian Forest

RESKA

Marshes
olation

Lake
Karellis

Lake
Tyrellis

Scion 2

Lakes of Varelle

Goreth · Borag

Silveria River

Lake
Nykarellis

· Garethe

A
reen way

The Deep
Fen

Grey Mountains

Tobel

Bay of Kyláron

· Varelle

The Burnished Mountains

Darrow

ckvale

Jade Hills

Sea of Vespers

East Goral

ra

· Tarwood

Bedlington

prologue

In an upper storey chamber in the ancient city of Darrow, Professor Leopold Taras rose from his desk and bowed his head graciously. 'Once again, I regret that I was unable to assist you, Mr Le Faye,' he said. As he watched his visitor leave the room, the kindly look in Taras's eyes slowly faded and was replaced by an expression of dark desire. 'Le Faye.' He frowned. 'It cannot be coincidence.'

The light footsteps of his guest could still be heard on the stairs when another figure entered the room and stood quietly in the shadows. Lean, with slender twitching fingers, he carried a solid walking cane, which he tapped against the rich carpet.

'Well, my friend,' Taras said softly. 'This has been a day of surprises. I've just been shown something of great interest.'

The newcomer stepped forward and in his eyes there was a cold, eager light. 'Sounds like something's brewing,' he said.

'Something most assuredly is,' Taras replied. 'Moments ago you would have passed a creature on the stairs. He possesses an object that by rights should be mine. It is a singular disc of stone,' he continued, his long curved claws drawing tightly together. 'The creature has it somewhere and though he is ignorant of what it is, he will guard it closely. Follow him until I can join you. Inform me of his whereabouts. And do not lose sight of him.'

The figure nodded and quickly left the room.

Taras stared down through the high window. In the late afternoon light a black ferret could be seen crossing the paved courtyard below. Some minutes later a second figure followed, his features obscured by a wide brimmed hat, his long shadow falling in dark ribbons across the flagstones.

CHAPTER ONE

The Meeting

The narrow cobbled road descended steeply towards the port of Bedlington. Jock adjusted his scarf, thrust his paws into the deep pockets of his heavy velvet jacket and moved steadily in the direction of the docks.

In the distance he could see the ocean, a strip of grey under an almost equally dark sky. As he pressed on, the ocean was temporarily lost to view, obscured by the angular roofs of the many ancient buildings clustered around the waterfront.

Lying at the bottom of the hill was a network of tiny alleys and narrow passageways—dark, unwelcoming places best avoided come nightfall. Old warehouses, mostly connected with the trade of the sea, hovered above the sprawl of paths and dim doorways.

Jock turned into one alley that led, after a few unpredictable twists and turns, to a large courtyard where the markets were held. The gloomy skies had kept some folk away; nevertheless the place was all bustling commerce, filled with makeshift wooden stalls, wheelbarrows, small canvas tents and several large embroidered marquees. Some of the merchants were regulars who lived by their trade. Others were strangers passing through, and it was often in the wares of these travellers that one could unearth the rarest items. More than once Jock had discovered some trinket or other that he carried home proudly, satisfied that he had a true bargain. Today, however, his mission was practical. He wanted a couple of decent fish for his lunch and a new hat for the wintry days ahead.

He made his way past a long table where two warthogs were attempting to barter with a gaunt and stern-faced ermine. A regular at the markets, the ermine was known throughout Bedlington for two things: the superb quality of his bellfire, a pungent and peculiar-looking spice brought from Asrain, across the Sea of Vespers; and for his absolute refusal to lower his prices under any circumstances. The hogs snorted in frustration, stamping their hooves hard on the cobble-stones and swaying their tusks from side to side.

'Bartering *is* the custom,' one of them grunted. 'Everybody barters—no?'

'I *never* barter,' the ermine replied softly, shifting his gaze from one hog to the other.

Jock wandered past the arguing trio and breathed in the dark odours of the bellfire. It was an argument he'd witnessed many times. The warthogs could take as much time as they liked cajoling, hectoring and pleading with the ermine, but in the end they would pay his price, for nowhere else would they find the spice as fresh and richly scented.

As he ambled towards the centre of the markets, Jock found himself momentarily distracted by the temptation of some pulpy yellow fruits that lay glistening on a raised glass tray at a nearby stall. He suddenly had to stagger backwards to avoid being run down by a river otter pushing a wheelbarrow through the crowds.

'Watch where you're going, oaf-foot,' the otter called over his shoulder, sniggering as he passed.

It was said that river otters bore some relation, distant or otherwise, to weasels—a view Jock had never shared. He'd met many otters in his time and had found them to be obnoxious and brash. A shame, then, that they were usually the suppliers of the finest fish one could buy, and Jock noted ruefully that the otter's barrow was filled with gleaming rainbow trout.

He sighed and walked towards a shabby stall, where a few limp herring lay in a small wicker basket. He scowled at the price displayed on the soiled card.

'After some ocean delicacies are we, sir?' asked the proprietor, a tall thin mongoose with a twitching mouth and deep-set eyes. He waved an oily paw above the fish and grinned wickedly. 'A grand weasel like your good self can hardly fail to see the quality of this lot.'

'I could buy a wee boat for that much!' retorted Jock as he thrust his chin towards the basket.

'Sir may be out of touch with today's market prices,' the mongoose snapped, his crude smile transforming into a contemptuous leer.

'*Sir* may be in the mood to give you a swift clout!' returned Jock before sauntering off to look elsewhere. 'Thieves and rascals,' he muttered under his breath.

He reached a stand where hats and gloves were strewn across a long table and noticed a soft brown velvet cap among them. He picked it up, placed it on his head and stared into a grimy mirror that stood at one end of the stall.

'Oh, now don't you look a treat!' gushed a passing gibbon. Jock grimaced, swept the hat from his head and was about to try another when he heard a loud voice yelling, 'STOP! THIEF!' He spun around to see a badger running towards him with what appeared to be an old canvas bag clenched tightly under one arm. He was using his other arm to shove folk out of his way, snarling as he did so. Some distance behind him ran a black ferret, and it was from this second animal that the cries came.

Jock stepped straight into the badger's path and swung a paw at his belly.

The badger gasped as he toppled forward onto the rough surface of the courtyard, the bag slipping from his grasp and tumbling away from him. Staggering quickly to his feet, he glared at Jock, the bag and the black ferret running towards him, then bared his teeth, let out a vicious growl and dashed off into the crowd.

The ferret was panting when he reached Jock, but managed to get out a word of thanks.

'Aye, well, it was my pleasure. I don't take too kindly to robbers running amok in these parts,' said Jock as he bent to pick up the bag, which had suffered little damage despite its rough handling. He thought that, given the abundance of fine jewels and spices to be found in the markets, it was an odd target for theft, for it was nothing more than a rough satchel, fastened by a pair of tarnished buckles. He handed it to the ferret, who held it tightly for a moment and ran his paw across its worn surface before slipping it firmly over his shoulder. Looking up, he said, 'Once again, thank you. I'm deeply grateful.' He stared uneasily into the crowd before continuing. 'I was busy leafing through a pile of old maps at one of those stalls when that scoundrel tore the bag from my shoulder.'

'Aye, well that laddie won't want to show his nasty jowls around here again. These stallholders don't forget a face quickly,' said Jock, rubbing his sore knuckles. 'So I gather you're new to these parts,' he added as he noted the ferret's exotic clothing: a heavy green coat embroidered about the collar with gold and copper thread, and around his neck a carved jade pendant.

'Yes, I arrived three days ago,' he said. 'I'm from Merrin.'

'Merrin,' said Jock slowly. 'That's near the border of Vareska, if my memory serves. You're some way from home—near forty leagues if I reckon it rightly.'

'Forty would be about right,' the ferret said. 'But I don't really notice the distance. I tend to travel rather a lot.'

'I wish I could say the same,' replied Jock, 'but I always find that something or other crops up to keep me here. Though that's not such a bad thing,' he added. 'You may not think it after your run-in with that badger, but Bedlington's a fine wee town.'

The ferret smiled and was about to reply when a deep voice called out politely, 'Excuse me, guv'nors.' A tall stoat bearing a carved wooden box passed swiftly between the pair. Jock glanced at the lid of the box.

'That's a nice bit of work,' he said.

'Yes,' said the ferret. 'It's a ceremonial goblet case— made by the Gorethian apes about five hundred years ago.'

Jock turned and stared at him with genuine interest. 'Is that so?' he said.

'It's the design on the handles that gives it away.' The ferret watched silently as the stoat disappeared into one of the marquees. Looking back to Jock he said, 'You did me a great favour stopping that badger. Perhaps you'd let me thank you by joining me for some lunch. I've a room in a tavern at the west end of the docks. The food's considerably better than one might expect, although the patrons can get a bit rowdy at times.'

Jock was hungry, now that lunch had been mentioned. 'Ah, you must be staying at the Ice Wolf.'

He laughed. 'Well, I'm quite accustomed to the goings-on of the docklands and I'd be more than happy to join you. By the way, I'm Jock,' he added, extending his paw.

The ferret shook it firmly. 'It's a pleasure indeed. I am Aramis, and it *is* the Ice Wolf, I'm afraid,' he said with a grin. 'Shall we head off?'

'Just a wee moment,' said Jock. He stared back at the brown cap, which still beckoned from the table where he'd left it. He reached for it, fished a few coins from his pocket and slid them across to the stallholder. Then he pulled the cap on.

Aramis looked towards the table and then glanced at Jock's cap. 'That would have been my choice also,' he remarked with a smile.

CHAPTER TWO

The ice wolf

They walked through the markets to the end of the courtyard, and after following the twisting lanes a short way, passed between two large storehouses and reached the docks. A wide wooden promenade stretched off to the left and right, and jutting out from this at regular intervals were six piers. All but one of them was empty. At the east end of the dock, nestled in the moorage slip between the last two piers, a coastal schooner sat, its sails furled. A broad gangplank had been lowered and a group of ocelots, clad in coarse grey tunics, were lugging heavy crates onto the pier, their harsh voices ringing clear across the docks in their barking, guttural tongue.

Jock and Aramis stood and watched them for a while before wandering down to the west end of the promenade. They walked past the empty piers in silence, occasionally casting their eyes to the bleak and murky sea. On their right, the warehouses gave way to rows of taverns, bed-sits and squat alehouses. Jock pointed to one of the taller buildings with an unusual facade of elaborate asymmetrical carvings. 'That's the Equine Guild,' he remarked. 'I'd steer well clear of it— it's where the horses go. Some spend all day in there, drinking that dark ale from troughs. Other races aren't usually welcome and most folk only go in when they have to hire a horse.'

'Yes, I know.' Aramis nodded. 'I've seen them coming and going—well, more coming than going, actually. Most of my journey south was by horse, as it happens. Quite a rough ride.'

Jock grimaced. 'It always is,' he said. 'I've *never* liked it! Sitting on one of those wee carts with their hard wheels, being dragged behind a great beast, every bump and groove in the road shuddering through your body. And then there are the horses themselves to deal with.' He pointed ahead.

Outside the Guild, standing near a line of stout oak casks was an odd-looking horse with wide nostrils and slightly bulging eyes. He was glaring at a large grey-feathered bird perched on top of one of the barrels.

'Now, Pyrrhus, old chap,' the horse was saying, 'you know I don't like to ask twice. Go on in and tell the captain that the ship is on its way.'

The bird casually unfurled a wing and scratched under it with his long curved beak. 'Tell him yourself,' he said before adding wickedly, 'Vicious Pete!'

'What? What did you call me?' the horse snorted in disbelief, his eyes bulging even more. 'You insolent, grubby avian!' He slammed his hoof hard into the barrel and the force of the blow split one of the boards.

'Oh, that was elegant!' Pyrrhus cackled, as thick velvety ale began to seep from the crack.

'In the name of the blue-tailed devil, what is going on out here?' called a stern voice as a second horse stepped out from the Equine Guild. The sight of the leaking barrel shocked him. 'The ale! Someone's paying for that!' he shouted. 'Own up! Which one of you chaff-grubbers done it?'

A clamour of indignant neighing and squawking erupted from the pair as each began accusing the other.

Jock shook his head slightly as he and Aramis passed by. 'That pair are always at it,' he said. 'But never mind.

Here we are.' They stopped at the door of the last building.

The Ice Wolf tavern was an imposing two-storey place constructed entirely from solid beams of black tapen-wood. These had been treated with the thick scarlet resin of the dewar plant, which had kept the planks remarkably free from the corrosive effects of the salt air and had given the inn a rich burnished appearance. There was a sign above the door depicting a large white wolf: its eyes glowing red, its jaws agape. Aramis heaved the door open.

Inside, the late autumn chill was soon forgotten. An imposing stone hearth on the wall opposite the door held a grate of smouldering embers and the air was warm without being stifling. A steep staircase beside the hearth led to the upper level. There was a bar the full length of the right wall and behind this stood the innkeeper, a wolf whose fur might have been white many years ago, but was now grey.

The tavern was empty save for a group of three otters seated in the far corner. They glanced up at the newcomers, but quickly went back to a game of chance they were playing with small cubes of coloured stone. On their table was a large tray of oysters, which they swallowed quickly in between throws before casting the shells into a wooden bucket on the floor.

The innkeeper shuffled out from behind the bar and seated the two animals at a small oak table below brass portholes that afforded them glimpses of the sea beyond. They ordered bowls of vegetable soup and two glasses of the tavern's renowned honey mead—a sweet but light beverage with a fine aftertaste. The old innkeeper went back behind the bar and disappeared into the kitchen. He emerged a short time later with their meals and, as they were both now extremely hungry, they ate in silence for a little while; the soft crackle of the fire blending with the low voices of the otters, occasionally broken by the clatter of shells falling into the bucket.

Jock raised another spoonful of the soup. 'This is a good thick broth,' he said quietly, 'and a nice change from cooking fish in my wee kitchen.'

Aramis nodded as he began to unbutton his coat. Under it there was a dark green weskit made of a soft glistening fabric, which caught Jock's attention. 'That's fired cotton, isn't it?' he said.

'Yes, it is,' said Aramis. 'It was given to me when I was up near Nardeyla late last year.'

'That's a long way north of here. If you don't mind me asking, is it your work that takes you to such places?'

The ferret leant back in his chair. 'It is,' he said. 'I'm an archaeologist.'

'Ah!' said Jock with a smile, 'an archaeologist. Well, this explains how you recognised that box in the markets. Now archaeology must be a fine line of work.'

'It certainly is. You might say exploring's the family trade.' Aramis stared at his paws for a moment. 'And what is it you do for a living?' he said politely.

'Well,' Jock began, 'I engage in a wee bit of work for the local constabulary from time to time and I've also been known to invent the odd thing or two.'

'That's an intriguing combination.'

'Actually, they go quite well together,' said Jock. 'It started a couple of years back when I crafted a small weather gauge for one of the local police lads. Before I knew it they were after all manner of things to help them with their work.' He laughed. 'It's not a bad living. But I'm sure it doesn't have quite the same air of mystery as your line of business.'

'Mystery?' Aramis fell strangely silent and an expression of unease settled on his features as his paw strayed to the canvas bag at his side.

Jock was watching. 'Are you still worried about that badger? He'll be long gone by now.'

'It's not just the badger,' said Aramis.

'What do you mean, lad?'

Aramis glanced first over his shoulder, then cautiously around the tavern. The three otters were completely focused on the tumbling cubes as they placed their bets in soft rumbling voices.

'Well, I'm beginning to think it may have been something other than a simple marketplace theft,' he said quietly.

'Why do you say that?'

Aramis hesitated. 'I think my room may have been searched yesterday while I was out,' he said. 'When I came back after lunch my compass was lying on a low table—but I was certain I'd left it on the bed. Until today I'd thought nothing of it. But now,' he said, laying his paw lightly on the bag, 'I'm not so sure.'

Jock leant forward. 'If you don't mind me asking, what's in it, lad?'

The ferret's keen eyes were fixed on a point somewhere far off through the small porthole. Turning back to Jock, he said softly, 'Something that I've discovered—something rather troubling. But we can't talk here. I need to find some new lodgings. Can you suggest another inn?'

'Aye,' Jock replied, 'there are several nearby—all much the same as this one, though.' He thought for a moment. 'I've an attic room I rarely use. If it's to your liking, you're most welcome to stay there.'

'No, I couldn't impose on you like that,' said Aramis.

'Don't be silly,' said Jock. 'It's no imposition at all.'

'Well, if you're quite sure, then I would be extremely grateful.'

'Aye,' said Jock. 'I am sure. In fact *I* would be grateful for the company.'

'I'll just head upstairs and collect my things, then.' Aramis rose from his chair and, after a brief exchange with the innkeeper, hastened up the staircase. Jock sat waiting and noted the way the proprietor's eyes followed the black ferret. Before long Aramis reappeared carrying an old battered suitcase. Jock got up from the table and joined him at the bar.

'Well now, let's take a look, shall we?' the innkeeper was saying. 'That's three nights, young sir, plus three breakfasts, two dinners and today's lunch—for two,' he added, peering at Jock. 'Now that comes to…let's see…four silvers, I believe.' He laid a paw on the bar and stretched out his long, twisted claws.

'Four!' exclaimed Aramis. 'Prices in the south are indeed *princely*.'

'Princely?' said Jock with a grin. 'You'd not find a *king* willing to shell out that much! It comes to two silvers and never more,' he said and glared at the old wolf.

The innkeeper's greying muzzle twitched before he replied in a husky voice, 'Right you are, Mr Weasel. Two it is. I must have done the sums a little quick, I'll wager, but no harm was meant, to be sure.' He rubbed his paws together and looked at Aramis. 'So *two* silvers that was then, young sir.'

Aramis placed two coins on the counter and the wolf dragged them towards him, his claws scratching harshly as they raked the bar's pitted surface.

CHAPTER THREE

New Lodgings

They felt the brisk sea wind sting their faces as they pushed open the wooden door of the Ice Wolf and began to walk back along the docks. The skies were growing darker as a wide band of swirling cloud moved in swiftly across the bay. Approaching them from the other end of the docks was a rowdy group of aardwolves, three of them howling an ancient sea ballad.

'Good afternoon to you, brothers,' one called as they passed.

'Aye, and to you,' Jock returned with a brisk nod. He made no eye contact, but kept walking with an unbroken rhythm. When he was certain they were out of earshot he muttered quietly to Aramis, 'Best not to dawdle near that lot.'

Aramis turned in time to see the group almost wrench the inn door from its hinges in their eagerness to enter.

'They fish off the eastern end of the beach, beyond the promenade,' Jock continued, 'and around this time each afternoon they stagger from inn to inn. Not bad lads, on the whole; just a bit spirited. But come late evening, you'll find them somewhat less cheerful than they appear in daylight. Yes,' he added, 'I've no doubt you'll sleep more peacefully at the other end of town. Speaking of which,' he said as he buried his paws deep in his coat pockets, 'why don't I show you the back way? We can avoid the market crowds and dodge that wind a bit.'

Aramis nodded and followed as Jock turned up a narrow alley between two of the warehouses fronting the piers. They took several more dim pathways before reaching a slightly wider lane of rather dilapidated shops. Most traded in food items sold from wooden barrels that littered the pavement. Jock stopped beside one of these and ran his paw through the dusty grain in it. 'You'd bake a poor loaf of bread with this lot,' he whispered. 'But there are a few gems—even in this part of town.' Having said this he paused before the next window upon which hung the sign, *Adeline Mirrow's Specialty Tea Shop*, then ushered Aramis inside.

The air within was heavy with the scent of rich tea and over it the faint aroma of honey and fresh syrup. Behind a scrubbed and polished wooden counter stood an elderly pine marten. She was weighing small hessian parcels of tea on a set of antique brass scales. Beside the scales sat a row of neatly tied and labelled bags, all bearing a detailed description of the beneficial properties to be found in each one. Aramis leant forward to inspect one of the labels.

'I'll be with you in just a moment,' said the pine marten warmly as she finished securing one of the packages with a short length of twine. 'Now, then,' she began as she looked up from her work. 'What can I— why, Mr Jock! How good to see you again.'

'Aye, and you too, Adeline,' said Jock. 'I couldn't pass by without a quick word. And I thought my friend might enjoy visiting one of the hidden treasures of Bedlington.'

Adeline laughed softly and turned to Aramis with a smile. 'Well, it's very good to meet you, sir.'

He returned her greeting, picked up one of the small packages and inhaled its rich aroma. 'This has a rather unique scent,' he said.

'Yes, indeed it does,' said Adeline. 'It's blue cassian, made from a very rare ingredient—kellris petals.'

'*Kellris petals?*' Aramis looked at the pine marten. 'Then, if I'm not mistaken, they must be harvested in the Madhra Hills, for I've heard there's no other region in Annistrelle where the kellris flower will bloom.'

'Well, there's not many around would know that.' She glanced at Jock. 'It is indeed a delicate flower and won't grow anywhere but the Madhra Hills. Folk say that when the flowers bloom—once every seven years— the hills are scented like honey and gleam with a pale blue light.'

'Well, I'm sold, then.' Aramis patted the counter. 'I'll take a bag.'

Adeline beamed as she took the little package from him, wrapped it carefully in soft brown paper and then tied it with a piece of old silk ribbon.

'Now you're spoiling him!' Jock teased.

'Nothing's too good for a friend of yours,' she said warmly.

Jock grinned and lowered his head before selecting a bag of his usual tea. He paid the pine marten and bade her farewell.

'Goodbye, Jock,' she called after him. 'And you too, sir,' she added with a brief wave to Aramis.

Out in the lane Jock said with a slight laugh, 'I think you just made a friend for life.'

They walked on past stores selling wicker ware, copper pots and exotic herbs gathered from places far beyond the shores of Bedlington. The air about them carried the mingled scents of crushed basil, cherry wine and musty cane, and from time to time fermenting berries and damp barley.

They left the lane and turned into a narrow alley that began to slope upwards in the shade of the warehouses. This soon intersected with the main street of Bedlington. As the pair emerged into the open, they felt the sea air whip against their faces.

Jock glanced briefly over his shoulder before tucking his scarf firmly about his neck and nodding at the way ahead.

Aramis stared up at the long road that would take them from the docklands. The quaint timber construction often seen in old portside villages was reflected in the buildings all around him. Tiny antiquated cottages with small well-tended gardens nestled close together on both sides of the street. As the road climbed steeply, these little dwellings gave way to taller and sturdier buildings weathered by constant exposure to the salt air and biting winter winds that swept up in icy gusts from the docklands. Many of the old iron gates and fences were flecked with rust and the paintwork on doors and shutters bore the marks of time.

'You've not been in these parts before?' Jock asked, puffing a little as he strode forward. Aramis shook his head. 'Well, it's not a bad little place. Once you leave the docklands it is like most other quiet seaside towns.'

They continued walking in silence for some minutes when Jock suddenly slowed his pace and, leaning towards Aramis, muttered, 'I believe we're being followed.'

'Followed?' whispered Aramis.

'Aye, I wasn't sure at first, but ever since we left Adeline's I've sensed someone creeping about behind us.' Having said this, he spun around. 'There's the dodgy fellow, darting off behind that building!'

Aramis turned to look, but the road behind them was empty. 'Did you see who it was?' he said.

'I caught a decent glimpse of him—it was a gibbon.'

'A gibbon?' said Aramis.

'Yes, and if I'm not mistaken, he's the very animal that insulted me today in the markets—the rude devil!'

Aramis kept staring back down the hill. '*A gibbon*,' he repeated softly.

'Aye, a tall brute. But there's no point lingering here now,' said Jock. 'He knows he's been seen and, besides, we've only a little further to go.'

They soon reached a narrow two-storey terrace with a polished wooden door and a gleaming brass knocker in the shape of a seahorse. Jock drew a heavy key from his pocket and turned it in the ancient lock. The door opened smoothly and the two animals entered a cosy sitting room. Aramis's attention was immediately drawn to a small mechanical device on a long side table. An intricate arrangement of springs and levers in it caused a metal bird to rise and flap its delicate wings while a silver pendulum affixed to the front of the apparatus swung hypnotically. A microscope and a neat pile of slides rested nearby, and beside these a peculiar pair of spectacles with a magnifying lens built into the left eyepiece.

'Is this your work?' asked Aramis.

'Yes, it is,' Jock replied. 'I've been making wee things for almost as long as I can remember. Those are the most recent,' he said, pointing to a glass case with eight compartments, each one containing a tiny animal carved from gemstone. 'I have to wind them every morning,' he added, 'but they run all day after that.' Aramis watched fascinated as a miniature bear made from a pale blue stone opened and closed its mouth, walked a short distance across the case on all fours, sat and then repeated the process. In another of the compartments a little giraffe raised its neck to an imaginary tree, made as though to eat, then lowered its head again. Its body, composed of a single piece of translucent crystal, had been hollowed out, and within was a minute clockwork mechanism. A tiny key set into its back turned slowly. The neck and legs had been carved separately and were joined to the body by fine wires, each no thicker than a hair.

'These are extraordinary,' Aramis exclaimed, bending to stare at the giraffe. 'I've never seen anything like them. Wherever did you learn to craft such detailed pieces?'

'My Uncle Fergus was a clock maker,' said Jock. 'He's retired now, but for many years he had a little shop and I'd often drop in and watch him at his trade. He hand-carved his own cases and he was always tinkering with gears and wheels. I think a little of his knowledge rubbed off on me.'

'More than a little,' said Aramis.

'I can't say that I've ever made a timepiece, though,' said Jock with a laugh. 'I think Fergus half expected I'd follow in his footsteps—this lot's a bit fanciful for his taste.' He rubbed his paws together briskly. 'Anyway, they keep me occupied.'

Aramis straightened up and saw that the rear wall of the room was entirely lined with books, many of them obviously very old. They were housed in a massive and heavily carved mahogany case and the titles that he could make out revealed an intriguing breadth of subject matter. Jock watched his new friend and sighed.

'Aye, it's taken me many years to assemble those,' he said, walking towards the high shelves and running his paws lovingly across the embossed, gilded spines. As he did so, he noticed Aramis ease his suitcase to the floor. 'Why, I've been a rather neglectful host,' Jock exclaimed. 'Going on about this and that while you've been patiently lugging your goods around. The room's at the top of the staircase. Go up and have a peep. It's not grand, but it is snug and has a capital view of the town.'

Aramis nodded his thanks and made his way quietly up the narrow staircase. He opened the attic door and stepped inside.

The room was furnished in soft blues and greens and on the walls hung two elaborate paintings depicting mythical scenes. One showed the legend of the Clouded Leopard of Sika calming the turbulent grey waters of the Sea of Vespers. The other featured more ominous figures drawn from a tale that had mesmerised Aramis in his youth and he was slightly surprised to find it hanging on this wall. There were three lizard-like creatures engaged in a great battle of sorcery. Strange eddying lights issued from their claw tips and the air around them was infused with brilliant streams of dazzling colour. Aramis gazed at the painting a long time before turning slowly to inspect the rest of the room. There was a small bed and a low oak dressing table with an earthenware pitcher and an oval looking glass on it.

Perched on a stand by the window was a long telescope trained upon the docklands and cobbled alleys through which he and his new companion had just passed. Beside the window was a hand-carved rocking chair and nearby a small table stacked with books. Aramis picked up one of the volumes and read the cover: *'The Art of Disguise by Dr T Baker'*. He opened the book and saw an inscription *'To Jock, with appreciation for your help in our latest conquest. Detective Ogitty of the Bedlington Constabulary'*. He put the book back on the table and, with a final glance at the paintings, turned to head downstairs.

It never occurred to him before leaving the room to place his eye to the telescope, so he did not see the lean figure glaring at the upper windows of the house before slinking into the shadows of a nearby building.

CHAPTER FOUR

strange stories

'How did you find the room?' asked Jock as Aramis came back downstairs.

'Very comfortable,' Aramis said. 'In some ways, it reminds me of my own home in Merrin.'

'I'm pleased to hear it,' said Jock as he busied himself with a pair of flints by the fireplace. In a few moments the dry kindling in the hearth caught the spark, and as the small flames curled about the twigs Jock placed several larger logs on top and prodded them lightly with an iron poker. 'That looks good,' he said, getting to his feet. 'Now I'll make us that tea.'

'Why don't we try this?' Aramis suggested, offering him the parcel of blue cassian from his pocket.

'Thanks, lad,' said Jock as he took the package and disappeared into the kitchen.

Shortly after, the two animals were seated in plush armchairs beside the fire, nursing mugs of warm, richly scented tea. Aramis, his canvas bag still slung across his shoulder, sipped slowly and watched in silence as one of the burning logs cracked apart and sent a shower of sparks into the air.

They sat quietly for the next few minutes, drinking their tea and listening to the wind as it played about the house.

Then Jock put down his mug with a contented sigh. 'Well,' he said, 'Adeline's always on the mark—that was a fine drop.' He settled back in his soft chair and looked at Aramis. 'So,' he said quietly, 'back in the inn you mentioned you'd made a discovery—something that troubled you?'

Aramis leant forward. 'I suppose I should begin with my grandfather. He was an archaeologist too, and a great inspiration to me when I was young. It was largely because of him that I chose the same profession. I grew up hearing the tales of his many travels. His name was Julius Le Faye—not a name that many would recognise, but in his field he was both well known and highly respected. It was he who discovered the ancient library of Kar-Teah.'

'Kar-Teah!' Jock raised his eyebrows. 'I've read about that—an ancient temple library, sunk deep beneath Lake Nykarellis. He discovered it?'

Aramis nodded. 'He did indeed, on one of his early expeditions. When he died, just over three years ago, he left his house to me—a small stone cottage on the bank of the Selann River. I've been living in it since then, although for the past couple of years I've been excavating a series of sites in the Marble Hills, so I've not actually spent all that much time there.'

Catching the shadowy light from the fire, his dark eyes seemed to hold a warm radiance. 'My work in the hills has turned up some interesting pieces,' he said. 'Antique vases, tables, even an ancient burial mound— but nothing quite as intriguing or disturbing as a discovery I made right in my grandfather's old home. Beneath the cottage there's a large cellar—a cool, dry place where he stored the strange mementos of his journeys. It was always my favourite part of the house and I used to spend many hours there as a child, playing with the masks and helmets and peculiar musical instruments he had collected.

'About a month ago I went down there to see if I could find a book to help me with some research I was doing. Grandfather had this enormous chest in the corner filled with all kinds of manuscripts and I started to go through them. The book I was after wasn't there, but right at the bottom of the chest I found an old silver box. And inside it was *this*.'

Opening his bag, Aramis drew forth something wrapped in several layers of faded black silk. Carefully removing these, he held up a thick disc of dusty stone, mottled with veins of black and deep crimson. As Jock peered closely at it he noticed a series of small indentations spaced evenly around the edge and, etched upon the surface, a row of fine symbols, like writing on a coin. 'That's an odd looking thing,' he said, sitting forward sharply. 'What is it?'

'I have no idea—but try holding it,' Aramis said, passing it to him.

As Jock took the stone his eyes widened. 'It's warm!' he said. 'As though it's been left out in the sun all day or heated by fire.' He stared at the disc and frowned. 'It feels unpleasant, though,' he said hesitantly, 'as if there's something—*wrong* with it.' He grimaced and quickly handed it back to Aramis, who set it on the table beside him.

'I've been unable to discover anything about it,' Aramis said. 'No one can tell me what these symbols mean. And I don't even know what type of rock it's made from.'

'I can't say that I recognise it either,' Jock murmured. He studied the stone for a moment. 'Was there anything else in the box?'

'Yes,' said Aramis, 'one other thing.' He reached into his bag again and drew out a small piece of parchment. He handed it to Jock, who took it in both paws and read in a low whisper:

Why did he have to bring this wretched thing to me? I knew it for what it was immediately, of course. As soon as I saw it I knew that the old legends of the Wain were true. There can no longer be any doubt—it is the Binding Stone.

What if some ill chance had delivered it to the Baron himself? Who knows what he might have unleashed?

I thought I had left all that behind. I thought I was done with the dark chapters of my life. But now this thing is brought to me and I do not know what to do with it. I shall put it away somewhere safe, until I know more.

'Was this written to you?' asked Jock.

'No. I think it's something my grandfather wrote for himself—in essence, a diary entry.'

Jock shook his head. 'But what does it all mean?' he said. 'What is a *binding stone*?'

'I don't know,' said Aramis. 'In fact, nothing in this note makes sense to me.'

Jock read the words again. '"*The legends of the Wain*",' he whispered. 'To me, that's the only part that has any meaning.'

'How is that?' asked Aramis.

Jock gave the note back to his friend. 'Well, you often hear stories about that region from the sailors in these parts. They're a superstitious lot, often given to wild yarns, and you never know whether to fully trust them. But they say the Wain is haunted and only the most hardened fishing crews will cast their nets anywhere near it.'

'Haunted?' said Aramis. 'By what?'

Jock rose, turned a log in the grate and stood for some moments staring into the fire. 'Nobody really knows for sure. Sailors speak of pale shapes that move upon the cliffs there.'

'What are they said to be?'

'That is where the tales gain their strength,' said Jock, 'for none can say exactly *what* they are. These tales have not been embellished in the way of most stories about odd encounters at sea. They all agree simply that these things move slowly upon the high ridges and then fade from view. To the sailors they are known as Ghost Wolves.'

'*Ghost Wolves*,' echoed Aramis. 'And you believe these stories?'

Jock turned from the fire. 'I can't really say. But creatures from these parts leave the place well alone. There's a ravine to the northern edge which separates it from the rest of the continent, and folk around here like it that way.'

He fell silent, sat back down in the old armchair and stretched his legs in front of the spiralling flames.

Aramis stared out through the front window and thought about what he had just heard. The sun's last rays faded and the street outside fell into total darkness for a few moments before the gas lamps flickered to life with a pale yellow glow.

Jock, meanwhile, watched the low flames dance as they etched constantly changing patterns across the logs. He found his eyes drawn once again to the disc of stone.

'Do you think it might be these Ghost Wolves that your grandfather writes of?' he asked.

'I cannot say,' said Aramis thoughtfully. 'But I hope I shall be able to find out soon. That's why I came to Bedlington. A very old friend of my grandfather's moved to this town many years ago. I have never met him, but I heard my grandfather speak of him often, and always with great warmth. I thought that if anyone could understand the strange things in the note it would be him. A fellow by the name of Milton—he lives down near the water in a lighthouse. I've knocked on his door a few times over the past couple of days, but it seems he's not at home.'

'That doesn't surprise me!' exclaimed Jock. 'I know Milton—quite well, in fact. I play chess with him every second Thursday, although I've never won a game.' He grinned slightly. 'Not in fifteen years. I'd wager he most likely *has* been at home, you know. He's—well, he's a singular chap. He's not particularly trusting of strangers, nor inclined to answer his door. But I'll introduce you, if you like. We can go tomorrow. It will have to be after lunch, though. Under no circumstances would you find Milton awake before midday!'

'It seems that I am in your debt once again,' Aramis said, smiling warmly.

38

'Think nothing of it, lad. But now,' Jock said, rising from his chair and rubbing his paws together briskly, 'I don't know about you, but I'm feeling rather hungry. Time for some dinner, I think.'

'That sounds good,' said Aramis. He picked up the disc of stone carefully and, after wrapping it in the silk, slipped it back into his bag.

As the two animals left the warm sitting room and headed into the kitchen, a dark figure who had been lingering outside the window adjusted the tilt of his hat and pondered all that he had seen and heard. Startled by the sudden sound of hooves, he drew back into the shadows as a pair of horses passed by. He watched them for a moment through narrowed eyes. In his hands he held a thick walking cane and his long fingers tapped noiselessly upon its handle, which was sculpted into the likeness of a bird's curving beak.

The street was now deserted and almost silent, save for the distant mournful call of the night gulls. With a final glance through the window of Jock's house, he stepped away.

An observer would have noticed nothing more than a tall gibbon dressed in a somewhat dapper fashion making his leisurely way down to the docklands.

●

'That wasn't a bad stew, if I say so myself,' said Jock as he shifted in his chair and stretched his legs out again. The dishes were cleared away and they had returned to the sitting room where several old books now lay spread out on the table before them. Aramis was leafing carefully through a thick volume with finely detailed etchings of fabled creatures. As he studied them he glanced up briefly and saw that his friend's eyes were beginning to close. He smiled to himself and went on reading.

Outside there were the peaceful sounds of evening: the gentle rustle of leaves against the window and the muted note of a ship's foghorn.

When Aramis looked up again, the fire had burnt low and the clock in the hall was chiming eleven.

Jock stretched and yawned. 'Well, laddie,' he said, 'it's getting late. I might retire for the evening.' He got to his feet and placed a small log on the fire. 'Now, have you all you need?' he asked. 'There's extra blankets in the cupboard over yonder should you want them.'

'I'm fine, thanks,' said Aramis.

'Sleep well, then,' said Jock.

'And you.' As Aramis was accustomed to later hours, he stayed by the fire for some time after his companion had gone to bed. Among the books Jock had left on the table was an atlas, and Aramis spent the next hour turning its pages and reading through the names of the towns, small cities, rivers and mountains marked on the map of Ravenwood. But he found his eyes repeatedly drawn to the southern promontory of the continent where the blankness of the interior was broken only by two words stencilled in high gothic script: *The Wain*. Closing the book uneasily, he put it back on the shelf and after packing up his case of belongings, slowly trod upstairs to his little room.

Elsewhere, as Aramis was preparing for bed, the innkeeper at the Firebird Tavern kept a cautious eye on a newcomer to his establishment. The Firebird was not one of Bedlington's finer ale-houses. It was little more than a dark, low-ceilinged common-room, brightened only by a great bird crowned in orange flame which had been painted on the back wall. Its clientele tended toward the shady, but Borek, the mandrill who owned it, had little objection to such types. After all, they drank often and paid readily. Besides, he reasoned, it wasn't his place to judge.

The crowd this evening was for the most part what Borek termed normal. A trio of sickly-looking stoats huddled around the fire drinking mulled wine and talking in low voices, while in the middle of the room a group of otters and ocelots exchanged fanciful stories of their adventures as they swilled from great tankards. Seated in other shadowy spots about the inn were the regulars who came most nights to drink and scheme.

And then there was the black cat. Borek frowned as he peered at her surreptitiously. She had arrived alone and taken a seat in the Firebird's only booth. This was generally reserved for large groups, but she had ignored Borek's pointed suggestion that *madam* move to a smaller table, and glanced at him with disdain when he told her gruffly that tonight's supper was a choice of onion stew or cornbread.

'No supper? Fine. Perhaps madam would care for a refreshment?' Borek had asked with a slight smile that vanished when the cat suddenly raised her head and stared at him. As he looked into her unblinking green eyes he felt a shudder pass through him. His profession had compelled him over the years to become a fairly shrewd judge of character and this was clearly not an individual to be trifled with.

Muttering something to the effect of 'suit yourself', he had retreated to his bar and watched her as he went about his business. That was an hour ago and in that time she had neither spoken nor moved.

The cat, for her part paid the innkeeper no further attention. She sat upon the tattered cushions, her back straight and her eyes fixed on the front door.

As she waited, she recalled the words of her employer some days earlier. The Baron had called for her unexpectedly and had seemed strangely intense as he spoke. 'Philios sends word that the ferret has travelled to Bedlington. I want you to go there—I will follow later.'

And so she had journeyed south.

Suddenly the inn's door was flung open and a gibbon carrying a metal-tipped cane strode into the room. He was dressed in a long coat, loosely belted across the waist and on his head was a felt hat with an unusually wide brim. He cast a look about the tavern and, rather to the surprise of the innkeeper, headed straight across to join the cat.

Borek nodded. 'Evening, Mr Charon. Enjoying your stay in town, sir?' he said.

The gibbon ignored him. 'A carafe of wine, innkeeper,' he said curtly. 'And some cheese.' He dropped his cane and hat on the seat beside him and waited in silence as Borek brought his order. When the mandrill had returned to the bar, the gibbon picked up a hunk of the pungent cheese and bit into it greedily. 'By the bloated goose of Goreth,' he said, 'I'm hungry now.'

The cat wrinkled her nose slightly and frowned. 'Well, do you have it, Philios?' she asked in a voice so clear and beautiful that it might have come, not from a creature of flesh and blood, but rather an instrument made from some ethereal, spidery metal.

The gibbon scowled and drank noisily. 'No, Lady Nefertiti, I don't,' he replied.

'So what happened?' she said.

Philios chewed thoughtfully. 'A weasel happened, oddly enough,' he began. 'I'd searched the ferret's rooms and come up empty so I knew he kept the piece on him. I was pretty sure which bag he had it in, too. He went to the markets this morning, so I figured it was as good a time as any. I found a surly-looking badger lurking around the docks and I offered him a few coins for a bit of thievery. He was all for it and made off with the ferret's bag, easy as you like.' Philios drained his glass and refilled it from the carafe. 'As he was running away, this hefty weasel jumped out of the crowd and socked him in the gut. Next thing I know, the ferret and the weasel are all buddied up.'

Nefertiti raised an eyebrow and studied Philios coolly. 'And that was this morning, was it?' she said

44

with an indifferent glance at the small clock above the fireplace.

'Bit harder dealing with two,' the gibbon said rather defensively.

'Well, the odds are more than matched now,' she said, her eyes slowly scanning the room. 'The Baron arrives tomorrow.'

'He's on his way, then?'

'By ship,' the cat replied and she stopped as she saw the suspicious face of Borek.

CHAPTER FIVE

The past meets the present

Aramis was roused by the early morning light filtering through the half-closed shutters of his room. He slipped out of bed and padded sleepily across to the dressing table. He filled a large shallow bowl from the pitcher, cupped his paws and splashed his face. The chill of the water jolted him awake. He dressed quickly and, after straightening and smoothing the bed cover, picked up his satchel and headed downstairs.

'Perfect timing!' Jock called. 'Breakfast's ready.'

Aramis set his bag down on a chair and wandered into the kitchen. The windows were open and a soft breeze was bringing in the crisp sea air. Jock had set two places. 'Have a seat, lad,' he said as he turned and lifted a large iron pan from the stove. He held his head over the pan for a moment and inhaled deeply. 'Yes, perfect timing,' he said. 'These are just as they should be, though I say so myself.' Aramis sat and Jock took a pair of tongs and placed two fried kippers on the plate before him. 'There you go,' he said proudly. 'See how you fancy that lot!'

Aramis took a small bite. 'They're delicious,' he said as he tucked in.

Jock sat down opposite him. 'I'm glad you like them,' he said. 'Here, try some of these.' He pushed a bowl across the table. 'They're rock pears, always in season. You wouldn't think so from the name, but somehow they taste just right with fish.' With his mouth full, Aramis took one and mutely nodded his thanks. Jock grinned and set to eating his own breakfast with relish.

After they had finished, Jock cleared the table and lifted an ancient grinder down from the shelf. He took a small pod from a jar and tapped it sharply against the bench several times until it split open and revealed a cluster of dark beans. Dropping a handful of them into the machine, he began to turn the handle.

'What are you up to there?' Aramis asked.

'Ahh, you'll see,' said Jock, looking over his shoulder. 'This is the best part.' He busied himself for the next few minutes heating a pot of milk and mixing the finely ground beans with brown sugar. Finally he placed a steaming mug before Aramis, and sat down with a mug of his own.

'Go on, try it, lad. It's home-brewed hot chocolate and I'll wager you've not had *that* before.'

'No, I have not,' said Aramis, picking up his mug and sniffing at it. He took a sip. 'You're right,' he said, 'this is definitely the best part.'

The two animals drank quietly and enjoyed the contrast between the breeze coming in from outside and the dying warmth of the stove's embers.

After they had finished, Jock rinsed the dishes, then closed and latched the kitchen shutters. 'Right,' he said. 'We've a little time to ourselves before Milton wakes, so we can wander along the docks and see what folk are up to today.'

Aramis slung his satchel firmly across his shoulders and they made their way from the house and down the steep road, Jock glancing behind them once or twice as they walked along.

'When did you first meet Milton?' asked Aramis.

'Let me see,' said Jock, 'probably fifteen years ago—though I'd heard of him before we had any dealings. I was fishing alone off the beach one afternoon when this crusty looking character hobbled up to me carrying a great armful of driftwood. "Can you give me a hand with this lot?" he asked. I said I would and before I knew it I was lugging not only all that he was holding, but several other solid pieces he kindly added as we crossed the sand.'

'All the way to the lighthouse?' said Aramis with a smile.

Jock nodded. 'Aye. And that was the beginning of a strange friendship. I remember walking into his room later and admiring the view, then casually commenting on a chessboard he had on his table. Before I knew it the old devil had challenged me to a game. He put on a slightly distracted air, but I knew within a short time that this was a very sharp character indeed.' He laughed.

They wound through the back alleys down to the promenade and along the waterfront. The docks were busier than they had been the day before. Three new schooners were moored in the slips and a variety of creatures were moving about, unloading boxes and barrels and dragging heavy cartons and chests along the thoroughfare. The air was filled with the sounds of ropes creaking and straining and the voices of animals exchanging news and gossip.

They passed a pair of otters struggling with a bulky cane basket that smelled strongly of vinegar and oil. 'Be careful, Janus,' one muttered nervously. 'You know if we drop this lot it'll be the whole month's wages gone just like that!'

'The only way *I'll* be losing a month's wages is in the Ice Wolf tonight,' the other one growled.

'Lucky you had a spare room,' Aramis whispered as the otters moved off.

A mandrill rolling a huge cask paused and drank deeply from a flask that was slung about his neck. Wiping his mouth on his forearm, he grinned brazenly at Jock and Aramis. 'Tis mighty thirsty work, lads, make no mistake,' he said, laughing.

'Aye, I've no doubt it is.' Jock nodded with a hint of a smile.

They headed west further along the waterfront, occasionally turning to look at the exotic produce that had just come ashore. In one wooden crate they saw small gauze packages, each bearing the distinctive golden emblem of a coiled salamander.

'Smell that bellfire,' said Jock, his nostrils picking up the warm, thick scent. 'The very best there is.'

'Ay, Jock!' yelled a rough voice.

Jock whipped round and saw a large cream terrier leaning against the rail of a small tug anchored nearby. 'Oh, hello, Angus!' he called back.

'Where you off to, then?' the terrier asked before biting into a huge hunk of bread.

'Round to the old lighthouse.'

'Chess, is it?' the dog said as he chewed slowly. 'The luck of some.'

'Yourself?'

'Up the coast. A bit of work off Darrow.'

'Aye, well it'll be nice and chilly up there.'

A dull bell rang and the terrier cast a look over his shoulder. 'That'll be us going,' he said as it rang again. 'Enjoy your day, lads!'

'You too, Angus,' said Jock. He leaned in close to Aramis and said quietly, 'He's a fine lad. Run into him every six months or so when the boats bring him back this way. Bought some decent tools from him last time he was in town. A more sensible fellow you couldn't find and yet,' he said, lowering his voice even further, 'he's one of the chaps who has spoken of the Ghost Wolves.'

Aramis looked back at the tug, which was just beginning to move out from the dock. The terrier was still on deck and waved briskly when he caught Aramis's eye.

'Good luck!' he shouted.

Aramis waved back and pulled his collar tightly about his throat as he and Jock went on their way.

Some distance past all the dockside commotion, the heavy timbers of the promenade gave way to an outcrop of flat rock that extended into the sea. There was no one about and the two friends enjoyed the feel of the smooth rock under their feet and the sound of the waters lapping and swirling around them as the waves fed little crevices and rockpools. They stepped over many of these, gazing down into the tepid waters where tiny red crabs scurried about, their little claws grasping at the swaying plankton while swollen starfish floated idly nearby, spinning slowly.

Before long they had passed over the outcrop and were standing on a large beach. On the far side a long headland stretched out into the bay and at its furthest tip there rose a great lighthouse, its white walls mottled with grey patches where the paint had worn away.

'That was once the saving grace of many a ship that passed through these waters,' said Jock as he drew his coat tightly about him. 'It's not been in use for many years. The trade routes changed over time and most of the cargo vessels these days approach Bedlington from the east—bringing goods from Tobel and Darrow. So the lighthouse at Cleggis Point is the main beacon in these parts now.'

'And has Milton always lived there?' asked Aramis as he stared ahead.

'As far as I can make out.' Jock thought for a moment. 'I can't remember him being anywhere else.'

'It must be a quiet life.'

'It seems to be to his liking,' said Jock. 'Mind you, he's pleased enough to see me for a game of chess, but he's also pleased to send me on my way again when it's over. Then he can settle back into his books and his port.'

They continued across the beach and climbed a rough path that wound in a thin trail around the headland. On either side grew clumps of stunted trees, their sallow leaves flapping in the wind. They soon reached the base of the lighthouse where they were confronted by a faded wooden door.

'This is closed but never locked,' said Jock as he turned the handle and pushed the door open. Entering a dim circular room, they gazed at the stairway that curved steeply up around the whitewashed walls. The stone floor was littered with broken shells, sea-smoothed pebbles and pieces of bleached driftwood.

'Come on,' said Jock, 'his room's halfway up.' As they climbed, Aramis looked at the small paintings that were hung at irregular intervals. They were portraits of old sea captains with greying muzzles and grizzled expressions. Other nautical mementos dangled from wooden hooks that had been driven into the walls: an old sextant, two worn flags and a rusted ship's bell. Jock stopped briefly beside the bell. 'I use this as a courtesy signal to let Milton know I'm on my way up,' he said and rang it twice. Then he signalled for Aramis to follow.

They stepped from the staircase onto a tiny landing where a door ahead of them hung slightly open.

'Come in,' a raspy voice called, before added wearily, 'if you must.'

They passed through into a room that was dark and far too warm for either of them, even on a day as chilly as this. The great fire burning in the hearth cast long flickering shadows across the walls. In front of the fireplace was a copper screen, and near it a tarnished copper trough in which a bank of squat logs had been piled. The screen was apparently less than adequate, for the woollen rug before the hearth was covered with black spots. An old, bespectacled sloth reclining in a deep armchair eyed Jock and Aramis with disinterest. 'Oh, it's you,' he grunted, squinting through his thick glasses.

'Aye. Hello, Milton old chap,' said Jock merrily. 'No no, don't get up, don't get up.'

'I had no intention of doing so,' the sloth said bluntly. 'Who did you bring with you then, eh, Jock?' He peered at Aramis.

'This is my friend, Aramis.'

'It's a pleasure to meet you,' Aramis said politely.

Milton sniffed. 'I'm guessing that it isn't,' he said. Aramis opened his mouth to speak, but shut it again at a knowing look from Jock. Clearly this was normal behaviour for the sloth and nothing to be troubled by.

'You've got your days wrong, Jock my lad,' said Milton languidly. 'Our game's next Thursday— although, if you've brought a bottle of port,' he grinned, 'I'll be up for one now.'

'No, I didn't come for chess today, Milton,' said Jock. 'It was to introduce you to Aramis.'

At this Aramis stepped closer and extended his paw. The sloth straightened his glasses and stared at him before slowly shaking it. 'Aramis, is that right?' he said dryly.

'Yes. Aramis Le Faye.'

Milton's manner changed. '*Le Faye*,' he echoed softly.

'Julius Le Faye's grandson.'

'Jock,' said Milton, 'open those curtains, will you?'

Jock stepped over to the wide curving window and pulled on a braided cord. The thick curtains parted, filling the room with dull afternoon light.

Milton leant forward to study Aramis's face. 'Yes,' he said quietly, 'yes, I can see it now.' He looked out through the window at a wide bank of grey clouds stretching across the horizon. 'Your grandfather was a great friend of mine,' he said and turned back to Aramis. 'If my memory is correct, you followed him into the profession, did you not?'

'I did.'

'So what brings you to Bedlington, may I ask?'

'I came to seek your advice,' said Aramis in a low voice, 'in a matter connected with my grandfather.'

Milton shifted slightly in his chair, his eyes travelling uncertainly from Aramis to Jock. 'A matter connected with your grandfather,' he repeated. 'Well, have a seat and I'll see if I can help you.'

Aramis nodded and sat opposite Milton, who watched in silence as he began unfastening his bag. Jock moved away from the window and sat quietly to one side of the fire.

'I've come here to ask a very specific question,' said Aramis as he slowly drew the silk bundle from his bag and placed it on his knees. He peeled away the dark layers of cloth to expose the stone.

Milton jerked forward. 'Where did you get that?' he said.

'It was hidden away in the cellar of my grandfather's house,' said Aramis and passed it to Milton, but the sloth shrank back and shook his head.

Aramis frowned. 'This was with it,' he said as he took the piece of parchment from the bag and offered it to him. The old sloth took the note warily and read it in silence. He sighed.

'You recognise this stone, don't you?' said Aramis softly. 'And you understand my grandfather's words.'

Milton passed the note back. Then he said suddenly, 'Jock, how long have you known me?'

'Well, I was telling Aramis on our way here that it must be a good fifteen years.'

'And you've considered me a creature of reason, have you not?'

'Aye, I have,' said Jock. 'You have your ways about you, like all of us—but you've set me straight more than once when I've needed some practical advice.'

Milton smiled slightly, but without joy. His paws curved about the edge of his chair. 'Your opinion of me may soon change,' he said dryly. 'I knew your grandfather Julius very well indeed,' he said to Aramis and looked down at the stone. 'He was a fine friend— my very closest. But beyond that he was a good creature in all ways. Do not forget that.'

'What do you mean?' asked Aramis.

'There is something about your grandfather's past that you do not know. These *dark chapters,* as he terms them in this note, relate to something you may find hard to accept.' The flames curled about the blackened stone of the hearth. Outside the sky was growing heavier. 'Julius was a great archaeologist, but he had another interest that took him to faraway places. Over time he became involved with a small group who shared his secret passion—they went by the name of *The Order of Symara.*'

'What was this shared interest?'

'Magic,' said Milton.

'Magic?' echoed Aramis. 'I don't see why an interest in the old stories of magic need be so secret.'

'You do not understand me,' said Milton. 'The Order's interest was not in any way theoretical. Its members were *users* of magic. They quested after prowess in the art. They studied the ancient ways to acquire the knowledge that had once flourished on the continent. In short, they applied themselves to mastering the very powers that most creatures believe to be pure legend.'

Aramis tilted his head to one side. 'You are saying that magic exists?'

'I am,' Milton said firmly. 'And that your grandfather was adept in the arts of sorcery.' He turned to Jock. 'You think I've had one port too many or that age has taken my wits, do you not?'

Jock cast his eyes downwards for a moment. 'I don't think your wits have left you,' he said slowly, 'but what you're saying is very strange.'

Milton sighed. 'So it is and so it was to my ears when Julius first told me of these things.' He paused. 'But have you *touched* the stone? Have you felt in it a strangeness you could not account for? A warmth, perhaps—but not one that brings comfort?'

'We both have,' said Jock. The mottled surface of the stone caught the fire's reflected light.

'Then listen to me closely,' said Milton. 'That stone is both ancient and dangerous. This continent was once populated by creatures that knew the art of magic and used it to both better their lives and conquer their enemies.

'Julius delved into this lore and his study led him into the hidden world of the Order. They were, and indeed still *are*, a group who meet clandestinely to share their knowledge and further their skills. By day none of them speaks of its secrets. So it was with your grandfather. Even I for many years did not know of his other life, and it was only when he began to have reservations about the Order that he confided in me. He thought its power was becoming too great and that the initial purity of its quest was beginning to bow to much darker intentions. There was one figure in particular, this Baron he speaks of, who caused your grandfather much concern.

'Finally Julius decided to leave the group—a step not without risk. The Order was wary of his motives and for some time its members watched him closely. But your grandfather's quiet ways eventually saw him fade from their interest and he soon grew less troubled and settled down to a simple life where his past involvement became only a memory. That was some thirty years ago,' said Milton quietly. 'And then came this stone.'

He shifted again in his seat and looked about the room. 'It's getting dark,' he said. 'Jock, my boy, light that candle, will you?'

Jock rose and took a candle from the side bench. He held it briefly over the fire until the wick flared, then placed it on the low table beside Milton.

The sloth nodded and drew his jacket about him. 'Twenty years ago this stone was brought to your grandfather by a farmer who had unearthed the thing while tilling his fields. Julius knew it at once. He paid the farmer for it and carefully hid it in his house.'

'What is it exactly?' asked Aramis.

'It is a prison,' said Milton swiftly, 'a prison that contains a terrible creature.'

'A prison?'

'Yes. Created by a race of powerful feline sorcerers—the Elmasen—who dwelt on the Wain in ancient times. Through their arts these creatures were able to look into other worlds, strange places that could not be reached by ship or carriage, and from one of these dark realms they called forth a monstrous being and trapped it in *that* stone.'

'If what you say is true, why didn't my grandfather destroy it?'

Milton shook his head. 'To shatter the stone would release the creature it holds and it would then be unbound—unstoppable. No. You see, the Binding Stone was one half of a larger artefact. It formed the crown of a staff and when these two parts—the stone and staff—were joined, the wielder could both summon forth *and* control the creature within.'

'To no good end, I'd imagine,' said Jock grimly.

'And where is this staff now?' said Aramis.

'That your grandfather did not know. Until this stone came to him he believed all traces of the Elmasen civilisation had long ago been destroyed. Not even the Order of Symara imagined that these things were still in existence and Julius intended to keep it that way.'

Aramis looked down at the stone. 'Then this script is in the language of the Elmasen?' he said. 'Now I understand why no one could tell me its meaning.'

'Who have you shown this to?' Milton snapped.

'The stone? Well—no one. But I did try to decipher the script—I took rubbings of it to several specialists in ancient languages. But all were baffled by it.'

'*Who* were they?' Milton insisted, his frown deepening.

'Professors Cavers and Kent at Nardeyla and there was Professor Leopold Taras at Darrow University.'

'Leopold Taras! You showed these markings to Taras?'

Aramis nodded uneasily. 'Yes, just before I came to Bedlington.'

'You have made a terrible mistake,' said Milton darkly.

'What do you mean?'

'The *Baron* spoken of in your grandfather's notes and this Professor Taras are one and the same.'

'Indeed they are,' came a deep voice from the doorway.

CHAPTER SIX

The Baron

Jock, Aramis and Milton turned around. Standing on the threshold was a tall figure wrapped in a long travelling cloak, his face obscured by the shadowy folds of its hood. He stepped into the room.

Lady Nefertiti padded after him with fastidious steps and sat back on her haunches, her green eyes betraying only a flicker of curiosity; and behind her Philios Charon, striding out with his cane in the crook of his arm. Leering at Jock and Aramis, he tipped the brim of his hat and moved to stand beside the cat.

Jock and Aramis rose quickly to their feet and Aramis slipped the stone disc into his pocket.

'Aramis Le Faye,' the hooded figure said slowly. 'Grandson of Julius—the noted archaeologist and *sorcerer*.' His words were soft and compelling and as Aramis listened he recognised a voice he had heard only days before.

'I remember you, sir,' he said.

'And so you should,' the figure returned, sweeping the hood back from his head.

The creature who stood before them was of a species not commonly seen in the southern regions—a Serathian bear, a race by nature lean and muscular and known for their somewhat reclusive tendencies. His fur was entirely black, save for two characteristic streaks of crimson across the top of his head, and a third much wider strand under his chin. His age was difficult to estimate: there was no trace of white about the richly coloured fur. Of a long-lived species, he was possibly anywhere between thirty and ninety years old.

The cloak he was dressed in was commonplace, lightly woven from coarse grey wool and sold in all the eastern port towns of Ravenwood, but the clasp that held it closed was singular. It was made from gold mixed with powdered gemstone to infuse the metal with slender veins of rich purple and delicately fashioned into a raised claw cradling a full moon.

Aramis looked at him steadily. 'Professor Taras,' he said.

The bear nodded slightly. 'You may call me "Baron". Your grandfather did.'

'Yes, so have I learnt,' said Aramis.

'I observe you have a little of Julius's spirit.' Taras narrowed his eyes. 'Regrettably, it did not serve him better. He could have been great.'

'He was.'

Taras gave a dark smile. 'If it pleases you to think that, so be it,' he said, drawing his claws closely together. 'But now to more immediate matters.' He stepped forward. 'I should very much like to have the stone.'

Aramis hesitated. 'It is not yours to take,' he said.

The Baron frowned and turned to Philios Charon, who immediately sprang forward and placed himself before Milton's chair. Milton struggled to sit upright as Philios pressed his thick walking cane firmly against the old sloth's chest. The gibbon tilted his head to one side and glared at Aramis. 'The stone, *Master Ferret,*' he hissed.

'You'll not use your thuggery here,' said Jock, clenching his paws.

But the Baron cut across him. 'I think your old friend would fare better if *you* were to stand your ground, sir.'

Jock saw the bear pull back the sleeve of his heavy cloak. Strapped to his forearm was a brace containing a long dagger, its red hilt glimmering with a cold light.

'Do not try me on this,' the bear said dryly. Jock looked quickly from the dagger to Milton.

'Don't worry about me, Jock,' Milton gasped. 'I've met worse than these ruffians in my time.' As Milton spoke, Philios Charon pushed on the cane so that it thrust violently against the sloth's chest.

'Now,' said Taras impatiently, 'the stone.' He stared at Aramis, who did not move. The bear's long claws uncurled as he took another step closer. His voice was almost hypnotic. 'It would be best for your companions if you obliged me. Perhaps you forget who I am—*what* I am.'

'It would be hard to forget what you are,' said Aramis.

The Baron considered this remark for a moment then raised a claw. Philios Charon chuckled grimly and, sweeping the cane high into the air, held it poised above Milton's head.

A look of insane malice spread across the gibbon's face.

'No!' Aramis cried suddenly. 'Stop!'

The Baron lowered his claw and Philios relaxed his grip, the muscles in his arm twitching as he returned the cane slowly to his side.

The room watched in silence as Aramis carefully drew the disc of stone from his pocket and held it out to the Baron.

Taras took it eagerly. He cupped it in one paw and ran the other lightly across its etched surface. In his bearing and posture there was a powerful sense of self-control, but something in the set of his jaw and the gleam of his eyes hinted at a growing obsession, as though a hunger normally kept in check had now been allowed to go unrestrained.

'What was it you wanted to know?' he said, looking at Aramis. 'The meaning of this script, wasn't it? It is a single word—the name of that which lies within the Stone.'

Taras gave a dark smile, his paw straying to the clasp at his throat. 'And now, I shall bid you farewell, for I've a voyage to undertake. I thank you for your *assistance*.' He gave a brief bow. 'Come along Philios, Nefertiti.' Drawing his hood forward over his head, he turned and strode from the room. Philios Charon trailed closely after him, twirling his cane freely as he walked. When he passed Jock he smirked.

'Cowardly devil!' Jock growled.

Lady Nefertiti rose smoothly to her feet. As she did so, she glanced sideways at Jock and something about her expression suggested that she did not entirely disagree with his assessment of the gibbon. She padded silently from the room and a few moments later the slamming of the heavy front door below echoed up through the lighthouse.

Jock turned to Milton. 'Are you all right?' he asked.

'I'm fine.' Milton coughed a little and straightened his jacket.

'That was the Baron, then?' Jock grimaced. 'Such a refined fellow! I guess he can afford to be, with that gibbon about to do all his rough work.'

'The presence of the gibbon is a choice on his part,' said Milton, 'It is in no way a requirement. Do not forget he is of the Order. You noted the clasp about his neck? That was not decorative; it is the Crest of Symara. In ancient times it was the mark of those who quested after prowess in Magic. Members of the Order use it now as a symbol of their devotion to the study of the art.'

When Aramis spoke his voice was distant as if he'd been roused from a dream. 'My grandfather hid the stone from him for twenty years and I had to go and place it straight into his paws. I have undone all my grandfather's careful work.'

'Don't blame yourself, lad,' said Jock. 'There was little choice.'

'Jock is right,' said Milton. 'There's no sense in thinking what *might* have been. But,' he lowered his voice, 'this development is very bad indeed. Now that the Baron has the stone he will be consumed by the belief that the staff may also have endured. He will undoubtedly make for the Wain and seek to discover if this city of the Elmasen—Kryl-Gavesk I believe Julius called it—still exists. If the city stands, that is where he'll look first. And do not forget what he will have if the stone and the staff are joined. The stone is the prison, but the *staff* will give him control.'

'I don't forget,' said Aramis quietly. 'Nor do I forget how he comes to have the stone in the first place. I should have been more cautious. The responsibility is mine and it is clear what must be done. I shall make for the Wain, also.'

'Well, if you're heading to the Wain,' said Jock swiftly, 'you'll not be going alone.'

Aramis was surprised. '*You* will come?' he said.

'Try and keep me away,' said Jock. He rubbed his paws together briskly. 'I'm quite eager to get after them right now.'

Milton stared at him. 'What do you propose to do, Jock?' he said. 'Leave this moment with no provisions and head off to the Wain? In the dark?' The sloth shook his head. 'No, not even the Baron will attempt the Wain by night. He will wait until the morning, as you must. In any case, he will travel by ship, for that is the only practical way to get there, but you do not have one ready, do you?'

'Well, we can hire a ship first thing tomorrow,' said Aramis, 'and be on our way by dawn.'

'Then if you really intend to go,' Milton said, 'there is something you should do before you leave—*someone* in town you should see.'

'Who's that?' asked Jock.

'Jarvis,' said Milton. 'He has been to the Wain.'

'*Jarvis*,' echoed Jock, 'been to the Wain? That's hard to imagine. He scarcely leaves his shop.'

'It was many years ago,' said Milton, 'and his experience there was far from pleasant. He'll not be keen to speak of it, but you may be able to learn something from him. It is worth a try. Call on him early.'

'Aye,' said Jock.

Milton looked out through the window, where heavy clouds masked the moon.

'I'll fetch a light,' he said. 'You'll need one on your way home.' He got up from his chair, took an old lamp, lit the wick and passed it to Jock. 'Now, go home and get some sleep,' he said. 'And Jock, my boy,' he added softly, 'keep your wits about you.' Then he shook Aramis's paw. 'Despite everything, it *has* been a pleasure to meet another Le Faye. Your grandfather would be proud of you. I hope we shall see each other again under better circumstances,' he said.

As Jock and Aramis left the room, Milton walked slowly to the window. He watched as the two figures, faintly illuminated by the orange glow of the lamp, emerged from the lighthouse and worked their way steadily across the headland to the lights of Bedlington.

Then he gazed out grimly at the dark sea.

CHAPTER SEVEN

The Wain

It was scarcely past dawn when Jock and Aramis left the house. Shouldering their packs, they began the steep descent down the main road. The street was quiet and, given the plumes of smoke rising from the chimneys of many houses, clearly most folk were still indoors, warm by their fireplaces. A cart filled with bulging hessian sacks rattled along, drawn by a grumbling, snorting pony, but the two friends passed no other animals.

Weaving silently through the back lanes they soon came to the docklands. A faint mist drifted upon the water and along the promenade a small crew of stoats had gathered to unload wares from a barge newly arrived in port. Other ships could just be seen approaching, their prows slowly emerging from the thinning haze.

'Jarvis is just a little further down here,' said Jock as he pointed to the eastern end of the quay.

They walked along the waterfront and halted before a heavy oak door in the side of the last warehouse. The door had been strengthened with thick iron bands, but Aramis noted with surprise that it had no handle.

Jock knocked sharply. 'What do you want?' a muffled voice snarled. 'I'm busy.'

'Open the door, Jarvis. We're here to buy water,' said Jock tersely. After a long wait a panel in the door slid back and a pale eye glared out balefully at the two friends.

'Oh, it's you, Jock,' the voice said. The panel snapped back into place and the door was wrenched open.

A small, but heavy-set sun bear stood before them, holding a shallow dish in one paw; the other dripped with honey. 'Water, eh? Plenty of that here,' he said as he licked his paw. With a grunt and a shake of his head, he motioned for Jock and Aramis to enter. They stepped past him into a small, dark room partitioned off from the rest of the warehouse and stacked with wooden barrels. They were struck by the smell of many varieties of liquor, scents that seemed to compete with one another: brandies, ales and wines creating a potent and heady atmosphere.

Pushing the door shut with his foot, the bear looked at Jock and said, 'Haven't seen you in long while. Hungry?' He held the dish out to him.

Jock shook his head. 'No thank you, Jarvis.'

The bear nodded slightly and offered it to Aramis. Peering into it, the ferret noticed that the honey was flecked with black grit. But just as he reached out he realised that the pieces of grit were in fact spiny razor ants, so he dropped his paw and politely declined.

Jarvis grunted again and placed the dish on a table by the door. 'So, how much water do you need, then? There are two sizes.' He indicated a stack of barrels in one corner.

'One of the smaller barrels should see us through,' Jock said.

'One small water. Right,' the bear said. 'Nothing else? There's a mead come in from Tornel—and a fine brew it is.'

Jock looked at Aramis and cleared his throat. 'There is one other thing, Jarvis,' he began.

'What would that be?' the bear asked.

'I've heard you may be able to help us with something.'

Jarvis tilted his head to one side. 'Is it a special order? I've had several folk request Honeyed Port from Oldfield this past week. It's an expensive drop—but well worth the price.'

'No, nothing like that,' said Jock. He shifted slightly. 'We have to go to the Wain and we need your advice.'

Jarvis looked grim. 'You want my advice? My advice is don't go. I went with a friend—I came back alone.' He turned away. 'I'll fetch you that water,' he muttered. Heaving a small barrel onto his shoulder, he lugged it back and placed it on the floor in front of Jock. 'That'll be two coppers,' he said dryly, his eyes to the ground.

'Jarvis,' murmured Jock, 'I'm sorry. I didn't know about your friend.' He looked uneasily about the room. 'I only ask this of you because we have no other choice. We *must* sail there.'

'No other choice?' The bear ran his paw over his chin.

'I'm afraid not.'

The bear stared at him. 'I can't speak of what happened to me on the Wain. Not to anyone.'

Jock nodded silently, drew a couple of coins from his pocket and passed them to Jarvis. He jerked his head in the direction of the door. 'Come on,' he said to Aramis. 'We'd best be on our way.'

'Wait!' the bear said and sighed. The two friends turned back. 'About twenty miles north from the tip of the promontory there's a sheltered cove. Anchor some way off shore and row in. It's shallow and rocky all about the coast, so don't try sailing too near. From that cove you can scale the cliffs. There's no other way to reach the Wain by sea.'

Jock regarded him silently for a moment. 'Thanks, Jarvis,' he said.

Jarvis nodded and pulled the heavy door open. Aramis went ahead while Jock quickly gathered up the water barrel. He began to follow his friend from the room when he felt a paw on his shoulder. He turned around.

'Good luck, my friend,' said Jarvis. Jock gave a grim smile as he stepped out into the street. He heard the door close slowly behind him and the dull clank of a bolt being pushed back into place.

'I've never seen Jarvis like that before,' said Jock.

'That cove he spoke of,' said Aramis. 'Do you know it?'

'No,' Jock said. 'But now we have a landmark to look for—and that's something.' The sky was becoming lighter. 'Come on,' he said, 'let's get this boat.'

They headed further east, beyond the warehouses and storerooms, to a row of wooden shacks opposite a crumbling pier. Most of them appeared to be empty, but a low light burned in the doorway of one that was set slightly closer to the water than those around it. There was a rough hand-painted sign above the door: 'Boats for Hire.' Inside a hefty mongoose sat by the counter splicing rope.

'Morning,' the mongoose said as he gazed up briefly. 'How can I help you?'

'We're after a craft,' said Aramis, 'suitable for a sea trip.'

'A sea trip, is it? How long will you be needing her?'

'We can't say for sure,' said Aramis. 'A few days— perhaps longer.'

The mongoose understood. 'Depends on how the fish are biting, I daresay.'

'Something like that,' said Jock. 'And we'd like to leave right away.'

'Well, it'll cost you three silvers for as many days,' the mongoose said, as he continued weaving strands of coarse rope together. 'Plus another two silvers deposit.'

While the mongoose watched every move, Aramis reached into his jacket and produced a small pouch. He counted out five coins and placed them on the counter.

'Right,' the mongoose said as he gathered up the money and slipped it into his coat pocket. 'Come on, I'll row you out.' He stood up stiffly and led them out to the top of a wooden ladder that poked up over the edge of the pier. At the foot of it was tied a small dinghy. 'Down you go, my lads,' he said.

Aramis climbed down and eased himself into the boat. Jock wedged the water barrel under one arm and clambered awkwardly after him. The mongoose followed them and, after untying the boat, pushed off from the pier with one of the oars. He looked behind him. 'That's her just over yonder,' he said as he began dragging the oars through the water. Jock and Aramis could see a ketch up ahead. Its name was on a brass plate affixed to the bow—*The Manatee*.

'You'll find all you need below decks,' the mongoose said. 'Charts and extra fishing gear. And she has her own small dinghy, of course.' He glanced at the sky. 'Can't say what the weather will bring you, though,' he added cheerlessly. 'These mists hide both the good and the bad—but the fish don't seem to mind.' He took a long pull on the oars and brought the dinghy in beside the *Manatee*. 'Here you are then,' he said. 'Watch your step.'

Jock and Aramis stood up carefully and tried to find their sea legs as the dinghy rocked on the choppy surface of the water. They scrambled up a thick rope ladder that hung down one side of the ketch.

'Now I'll expect you in three days, my boys,' the mongoose called as he began to push off again. 'Or you'll be lining my pockets with extra silvers.' He grinned.

Jock waved and commenced unfurling the sails while Aramis dragged their packs below decks. He came back up, holding a tattered chart. He studied it for a moment, folded it and slipped it into his pocket. With a quick nod to Jock, he went forward to raise the anchor.

Released from her mooring, *The Manatee* sailed smoothly out from the bay to the dark waters of the Tyresse Ocean. A fine mist still hung over them and in the distance Jock and Aramis could just make out a fishing fleet.

Back along the coastline, the Bedlington waterfront now appeared as a miniature panorama with small figures moving among barrows, crates and rows of hessian sacks. They could hear the distant thud of planking being dragged to and from the vessels docked there and the tolling of a pilot's bell from one of the large fishing schooners moving slowly in to port. From time to time there came the muffled cry of a sailor's voice as the crews hauled in catches or cast fresh nets.

Further south, Jock and Aramis passed a large trading vessel coming in to port, with a flag indicating fine conditions ahead. 'There's a heartening sign,' said Jock.

Aramis came up beside him. 'We should reach the Wain around noon if this wind stays with us,' he said.

'Aye, well she's on our side now.' Jock nodded.

As they sailed on through the morning, their course took them further south-west. The mist gradually began to rise and the soft light of the sun bathed the waters below with dappled shifting patterns.

As Jock walked about the deck he was distracted by a movement in the water. Leaning over the wooden port rail, he saw a massive broad-finned fish following them.

'What is it?' asked Aramis, peering over the rail with him.

'A callert,' said Jock gravely. He frowned. 'The sailors in these parts say it's an ill omen.'

'I've never seen one before,' said Aramis.

'Nay, it's not a common sight. But on the docks you hear many a tale about this fish. All regard it suspiciously. They say if one dogs your craft you'd best take care.'

'I thought you gave little credence to the stories of sailors,' said Aramis.

Jock sighed. 'After everything that's happened, I'm not certain what I believe anymore,' he said.

By midday, the great promontory of the Wain came clearly into view. Eruptions of foamy white spray around the far-reaching fingers of land spoke of the jagged reefs and treacherous shelves that lay beneath the surface. Aramis scanned the coast, trying to identify the cove Jarvis had spoken of.

'Over there,' he said suddenly, pointing some way into the distance. Jock followed his friend's outstretched paw and saw a dark opening in the cliff face, as if an enormous bird had sunk a single claw deep into the sheer rock and ripped a piece out. Near the mouth of the cove a high-masted boat was at anchor. Jock quickly reached into his jacket and produced a small bronze spyglass. He raised it to his eye. 'It'd be his all right,' he said and handed the glass to Aramis.

'There doesn't appear to be anyone on board,' said Aramis. 'I'd say they've already rowed ashore.' He gave the glass back to Jock. 'Come on,' he said, 'let's get a little closer.'

As they sailed further in, Aramis kept an eye on the other boat while Jock looked for a suitable place to anchor.

'This should about do us,' Jock said when they were less than half a mile from the shore. Aramis nodded and they commenced to haul down and secure the sails. Then Jock lowered the anchor and it fell with a dull splash into the water. When this was done they both stood quietly for a moment and looked towards the Wain. A faint chill breeze blew about their ears and now that their boat was still, they were aware of a heavy silence, broken only by the occasional slap of a wave against the hull and the high calls of bellarc terns whose desolate rookeries lay in the southern seas.

'I'll get our supplies,' Jock said as he headed for the hatch and disappeared below.

Aramis remained standing at the bow of the ship. The upper contours of the Wain rose in sharp uneven peaks against the sky and as he stared at them, he thought for the briefest moment that something moved up on the high ridge. He closed his eyes and checked again, uncertain about what he had seen. The sound of the hatch closing behind him broke his attention and there was Jock dragging their two packs across the deck.

As he stepped back from the bow, Aramis glanced once more at the Wain.

'I've filled our flasks,' said Jock. 'I think we have all we need.'

'Good,' said Aramis. 'Then let's be on our way.' He took the packs from Jock and loaded them into a dinghy that was lashed to the stern. After they were stowed, he turned the handle of an ancient winch to lower the small craft into the water.

Jock did a final check that all was secure on board, then he and Aramis climbed carefully down the rope ladder. As Aramis began fitting the oars into the rowlocks, Jock untied the knot that held the craft securely to *The Manatee,* and cast off. Then Jock grasped the oars and began rowing towards the shore.

The waters about them looked discoloured, as though a dark stain had spread slowly from the land out into the sea. They grew wary as they passed by the high-prowed boat anchored closer to the shore than they had dared venture.

'It's an impressive craft,' Jock said grimly. 'This Baron is clearly not short of the coin of the realm.' He fell silent and continued to row with increased effort.

As they drew closer in they were struck by the majesty of the cliffs—sheer walls of dull grey stone some two hundred and fifty feet high. They seemed imbued with an implacable coldness, as though somehow immune to the sunlight that fell directly on them.

Both animals felt a peculiar disquiet, but they soon had more urgent concerns, for the pull of the waves was beginning to drive them off course. His eyes stung by plumes of salt-spray, Jock concentrated simply on getting through, while Aramis occasionally broke the silence with, 'steady' or 'hard to starboard'. Suddenly as the choppy waters surged against the boat, Aramis spotted a twisted crown of dark rock close to the prow. 'Watch out!' he cried. Jock spun round and felt one of the oars catch against the rock and drag heavily. He pulled on it frantically as the hull slammed against another part of the reef. The boat lurched and Aramis gripped the side as Jock fought to free them. A larger wave crashed against the side of the boat, swinging it round and driving it off the reef. Jock gave several powerful strokes on the oar, and then with Aramis guiding, they moved steadily away from the sharp rocks.

'That was close,' said Aramis. 'Are you all right?'

'Aye, lad. But I don't know if I can say the same for our boat. That was quite a whack she took. I'll check her when we get ashore.'

They finally managed to manoeuvre the dinghy into the mouth of the inlet. Once they had passed the opening, the waters became calmer and Jock rowed more gently.

'*The Wain*,' he muttered under his breath and rubbed at his aching shoulders.

They squinted as the sun shone straight into their eyes, but the inlet began to curve sharply around to the south-west and with another stroke the dinghy suddenly moved out of the light and into deep shadow. The channel gradually widened into a small dim bay, and craning their heads about, they could see before them a bank of dark sand flanked by boulders and rough pebbles.

A stroke or two later there was a harsh scraping as the prow ground against the bottom. Jock swiftly withdrew the oars and the two friends leapt from the boat and began to haul it up onto the narrow beach. The cold sea water, thick with coarse black grit, lapped around their legs as they waded through the shallows, and both animals found themselves relieved when they felt dry sand creep beneath their feet. They dragged the boat up behind a large boulder that lay above the water line and lashed it there firmly. Jock inspected its hull. It bore a jagged scratch, but no other damage. 'Well, she's still seaworthy,' he said. 'That's some comfort.'

A little way further along the beach, they saw a larger rowboat lying on the sand.

Aramis walked over to it and peered about the ground. 'Milton was right,' he called. 'They did not arrive here until some time this morning—you can still see their footprints.' He headed back to Jock and they collected their packs from the dinghy and turned to stare at the steep escarpment rising high above them.

Patches of the rock wall were deeply recessed and stained with dark shadows, and a thin salty film clung to the surface and glittered strangely in the faint light. Slinging lengths of rope about their waists, they adjusted their packs, looked up and began the steep climb.

They had gone only a little way when Aramis, grasping a narrow ledge of rock, said quietly, 'Have you noticed that the birds do not land upon these cliffs? I've watched them circling above us, but they soon soar back over the waters.'

'Aye, it is very odd,' said Jock, 'and not greatly comforting.'

Continuing to climb, they found that the upper part of the cliff was an almost sheer wall with few footholds. These appeared fragile and Jock tested the strength of each one carefully before calling down to Aramis that it was safe to proceed. Eventually he caught sight of a slight overhang extending from the very top of the cliff. 'Just a bit further,' he muttered to himself as he edged steadily upwards, his arms tired and stiff. Finally his paw curled over the top, and, grasping the edge tightly, he heaved his body up and over. 'Come on. I'll give you a hand,' he called.

Kneeling in the dusty ground, he bent forward to grip Aramis's arm and hauled him over the ledge. The two animals staggered to their feet and, after shaking the grit from their fur and clothing, turned and stared into the vast bleakness of the Wain.

CHAPTER EIGHT

The Grey Wasteland

Before them stretched a plateau of grey rock, its pale surface broken by wide shadowy groves of twisted trees. Dotted about between these were what appeared to be small pools of dark still water.

In some places the ground was cut with narrow fissures, like ashen veins spreading in fine spidery patterns across the land. A hushed, suffocating stillness lay upon the area, so heavy that neither Jock nor Aramis could at first speak without feeling that his voice might waken something that lay dormant among the stones.

Aramis surveyed the plateau, then turned his attention to the ground immediately before him. He studied this for several minutes, walking back and forth very slowly, before suddenly kneeling down and peering closely into the dust.

'What do you see?' whispered Jock.

'There,' said Aramis, indicating some faint scuff-marks. 'It's not much, but it *is* a trail we can follow, and that's a start.'

Pulling their jackets tightly about them, they moved on in silence, slowing from time to time to examine the trail. The rock beneath their feet grew colder and the air more stifling, as though the very silence itself was pressing in on them.

Accustomed to the constant sounds of dockland life, Jock found himself troubled by the stillness. As he looked ahead, he whispered, 'You almost wish for some familiar noise.'

No sooner had he spoken than there came a sound so faint that they were not certain they had heard it at all.

'What was that?' said Jock, turning his head slightly. 'Did you hear it?'

'I think so,' said Aramis. 'It sounded like something scraping against wood.'

They stood still, waiting to hear it again, but the sound was not repeated.

'Come on,' said Aramis glancing cautiously around him.

They began to move again. As they walked the ground became increasingly stony. Aramis slowed his pace. 'I can't find any sign of their passing now,' he said. 'Perhaps a skilled tracker could, but on this rock I can make out nothing.'

Directly ahead of them was one of the small pools of water and immediately beyond lay a grove of the twisted trees.

As they approached the pool they saw that it was about twelve feet in diameter, in the shape of a rough circle. The stones that surrounded it were bleached to a chalky, lifeless white. They looked brittle—those nearest the water's edge had already crumbled away into dust.

Jock and Aramis stopped a short distance from the pond and stared into it. The dark green water was utterly still and flat, as though it was not liquid but rather a sheet of flawless gemstone that had been laid across the ground, offering an emerald reflection of the cold sky above. Both animals felt a sense of disquiet as they took in the scene, a feeling that increased when Jock looked up and saw what lay beyond the far side of the pool. He touched his friend's arm and pointed.

They had not noticed the skeleton at first because its colour matched that of the stones. Neither Jock nor Aramis could identify the type of creature it had been. It lay stretched out on the white dust, its long claws clasped about a crumbling rock as if it sought to escape the water even in death.

'Some poor traveller, do you think?' murmured Aramis. 'Or perhaps one of the inhabitants?'

'Actually, I hadn't given much thought to the possibility that folk might live here,' said Jock softly. He looked about the Wain. 'I suppose it's possible, though.'

As they stood by the pool their sense of unease was growing and, almost involuntarily, they took several steps back from the water.

'So, which way should we go?' said Jock after a pause.

'Well, the last tracks we saw headed due west. If the Baron continued in that direction, then he would have gone in there,' said Aramis, indicating the grove.

'Then, let's have a look,' said Jock.

Aramis nodded. 'With some good fortune, we'll pick up their trail again.'

Circling around the pool, they headed across the stony ground and passed in among the trees. These were tall and ash-white, their limbs contorted and their sallow bark smooth to the touch. Small patches of dank moss clung to the trunks, giving off a subtle odour of staleness, as if a door to a long sealed cellar had finally been opened. Above was a dense canopy of leathery mauve leaves and all about them were pale branches, in places hanging so low that they brushed the ground.

'Have you ever seen trees like these on your travels?' asked Jock as he pushed through a tangle of foliage.

Aramis shook his head. 'No, nothing like them.'

The two animals walked on in silence, each scanning the ground ahead for some sign of the Baron's passing. After a few minutes, Aramis halted. He beckoned Jock over to him. 'Look at this,' he said, pointing to a place on one of the trees where the bark had been scraped away, as though sharp claws had torn into it. A small trail of dark scarlet sap dripped slowly from the wounded trunk and gathered in a small mound at its base. Glancing about, they noticed that another of the trees nearby bore similar scratch marks.

'It seems that the Wain has inhabitants after all,' said Aramis.

Jock nodded and was about to speak when a low voice whispered suddenly, 'Of course it does.'

The two friends whipped around. The grove was dense and secretive. Anything could be hiding among the sweeping branches and thick foliage. In those deepening shadows skulked *something* whose eyes were certainly at that moment fixed upon the two of them.

'All right, then, let's see you!' Jock shouted with feigned confidence.

There was a rustling and from behind a clump of trees appeared a peculiar creature. They immediately recognised its kinship with the skeleton. Gaunt and long-limbed, it was covered with black shaggy fur that was thoroughly dishevelled and dusty. It walked on two legs and with a pronounced hunch, although were it standing upright it would have been as tall as Jock. Its fingers were long and tapered to a fine needlepoint claw. Its protruding ears made its face seem small and the wide discs of its eyes betrayed neither fear nor concern.

It moved slowly towards Jock and Aramis, stopped a few paces away and studied them.

'Not many come wandering here,' the newcomer said. His voice was soft and cold. He scratched the top of his head. 'Not many come,' he repeated, 'and fewer still leave. You almost didn't,' he added.

Jock and Aramis exchanged an apprehensive glance.

'What do you mean, lad?' asked Jock.

'I saw you,' the creature said, 'near the Kailya. If you'd taken one step closer—' He made a nasty crunching sound in the back of his throat.

'The Kailya?'

'It means *deep wells*—the pools—like water, but not water. Bad places they are.' His face wrinkled up slightly. 'Although,' he went on thoughtfully, 'the elders say that maybe they are not really places at all, but live things.'

'Live things?' Aramis frowned.

'Alive and hungry,' the creature replied with a wicked grin. 'Some travellers get eaten. Some Aye-ayes too, if they don't take care.' Observing the expressions on the faces of Jock and Aramis, he pointed at himself and said, with unnecessary slowness, 'Aye-aye. What I am. My—race, I think you say?' He edged closer to the two friends. 'Why do you come to the Wain? Nobody comes here,' he said, without waiting for an answer, 'they have not done for a long time. Then suddenly two on the same day—you and, before you, the others.'

'You've seen others? Today?' asked Aramis swiftly.

The Aye-aye nodded. 'Yes, others. I saw—' He fell silent and tilted his head slightly.

'You saw?' Aramis prompted him.

'Quiet!' the Aye-aye hissed. He scampered over to a tree and, leaning in, pressed his ear to it. He closed his eyes and began tapping one of his long fingers against the trunk, pausing every few seconds to listen. Suddenly an expression of triumph crossed his face and jerking his head back, he began to tear frantically through the white bark, shredding it until he had made a sizable hole. With a snarl of satisfaction he stabbed a finger into the opening, and when he drew it out there was a fat twitching caterpillar impaled on the claw tip. He grinned at Jock and Aramis before stuffing the small creature into his mouth and chewing it loudly.

'Good food to eat on the Wain,' he said, chomping with his mouth open, 'if you know where to look.'

Trying not to let his distaste show, Aramis started again. 'You were saying you had seen others?'

'Oh, yes,' said the Aye-aye as he swallowed the last of the caterpillar. 'Three of them, but one was different—powerful, he was. They met another Aye-aye not far from here. I was watching—saw it all. The powerful one said he needed to find a place—he called it Kryl-Gavesk. Bah! That's the old name. The *dead city* is its proper name now.'

'So it exists, then,' Aramis interrupted. 'The Elmasen city still stands?'

'Of course.' The Aye-aye frowned. 'The powerful one said to show him the way to the dead city. The other one like me said *why?* The powerful one said because he would give him a reward.' The Aye-aye gave a strange chuckle. 'A *good* reward.'

'What did he offer? Coins and jewels, I suppose,' said Aramis.

'Jewels?' The Aye-aye laughed. 'Useless! What can we do with jewels? No, the powerful one—he is smarter—he *understands*. He told the gibbon what to do. The gibbon took out a knife and away he went. He hunted for some time—very good at it too, he was, and when he came back he *had* it.' The creature's wide eyes were shining.

'*What* did he have?' asked Jock.

'A whole bag of beetles,' the Aye-aye replied in wonder. 'A *whole* bag. How many? Twenty? Thirty? More, perhaps—and he didn't need to listen hard at the logs and trees.' He shook his head in disbelief. 'The powerful one said, "Show me the city and you get the bag". So off they went.'

'To Kryl-Gavesk—the dead city?' said Jock. The Aye-aye nodded.

'Listen, lad.' Jock lowered his voice. 'Do you know where the city is yourself?'

The Aye-aye narrowed his eyes. 'I know where it is,' he said.

'Could you tell us the way?' asked Aramis.

'It's a long way, too hard to tell. I'd have to *show* you.'

'Would you be willing to, then?' said Jock. 'It's very important that we get there.'

'I *could* show you,' the Aye-aye said. His grin revealed small sharp teeth, crooked and yellow. 'I could show you for the same price, yes?'

'I'm sorry, lad,' said Jock, 'we really don't have time to go searching for beetles. The bear—the powerful one, as you call him—is extremely dangerous. We must catch up with him. Please help us.' Noting the dubious look on the Aye-aye's face, he added, 'You'd be doing the right thing.'

The Aye-aye raised a long claw and scratched slowly at his ear while he considered Jock's words.

'I like to do the right thing,' he said at length, nodding his head vigorously. 'I will take you to the dead city. Kryl-Gavesk.'

Jock and Aramis paused, uncertain whether to trust this creature before them with the steady, unblinking eyes.

'It is this way,' he said, jerking his head to the west. 'Come, I will take you.'

He moved off and Jock and Aramis fell in behind him.

They travelled through the grove in silence for a few minutes, then the Aye-aye said suddenly, 'The powerful one is your enemy, yes?'

'You could say that,' said Jock, ducking under a low branch.

'And what will you do when you get to the city— when you catch up to him?'

'We are not quite sure,' Aramis admitted with some hesitation. 'He has taken something that does not belong to him and we must get it back. We need to stop him.'

'Stop him? Oh, I don't think so.' The creature glanced over his shoulder. 'No, there won't be any stopping *that* one.'

Jock and Aramis said nothing.

They followed the Aye-aye out of the grove and before long the land fell away into the gentle slopes of a misty valley. They crossed this carefully, the rock surface gradually giving way to patches of pale earth that sank under their feet. When they reached the ridge on the far side they stopped. Rising above them through the mist, pointing upwards like gaunt lifeless fingers, were four twisted spires of stone, their tall peaks finely silhouetted against the sky.

'What are these?' said Aramis. The rocks threw long claw-like shadows across the earth.

'We call them the Talons,' the Aye-aye said. 'Aye-ayes made them long ago. To warn away others.' He held up one of his hands. 'See,' he said as he raised his long fingers. 'But we don't stop here. We must go down there—into the Shen-vale.' He pointed.

The way ahead was obscured by thick white clouds across the land.

'It smells dank,' said Jock, sniffing the air with displeasure.

'Yes, dank,' the Aye-aye agreed with a nod. 'But we must go there if we want to reach the great Kryl-Gavesk. Come.'

As they walked down from the Talons, the air they were breathing became heavy with the mist. Soon the ground began to level out and grow damp and unsafe, the dark mud trailing sluggishly over their feet.

'Come, come.' With one of his long bony fingers the Aye-aye urged the two friends to catch up. 'The Shen-vale is near—and there's good eating to be had there.' They pressed on. The Aye-aye scurried ahead to wait as Jock and Aramis slogged across the muddy ground with greater caution. Soon they found themselves standing on a raised bank of grass overlooking a wide marsh. The mist completely surrounded them now and obscured everything more than a few paces away but, despite its chilly appearance, the air was humid. Their foreheads were beaded with perspiration and their dampened clothes clung uncomfortably to their fur. The Aye-aye seemed unaffected by this. He peered into the fog with an expression of pleasure on his face.

Jock frowned. 'Are you sure this is the only way?' he said. The Aye-aye looked at him sideways. 'Of course,' he said. 'These are the swamplands—we say Shen-vale. The dead city lies over the water.'

There was a hollow snap as a marsh bubble burst open close by and lifted a patch of fog from the surface as the foul gas escaped. Slender tendrils of vapour rose from the water like the fingers of some ghostly creature seeking something blindly by touch alone, before slowly fading away.

'It smells like rotting fruit,' Jock muttered, pushing his scarf up over his muzzle. A cloud of small insects, drawn by the scent, darted among the reeds, their thin wings buzzing loudly.

'Keep close to me. There *are* ways through the swamp,' the Aye-aye said as he sidled along the water's edge. 'See—not so bad?' He pointed ahead to a strip of rough grass, perhaps four paces wide that snaked out into the water. He stepped onto it. 'Come on,' he said impatiently.

The two friends followed him onto the marsh, but had not gone far when Aramis suddenly stopped.

'Did you hear that?' he whispered.

Jock tilted his head.

'I thought there was a rippling sound somewhere out in the water,' said Aramis.

'Just marsh gases,' the Aye-aye said with a languid wave of his hand. 'These waters are much deeper than they seem. Deep and dark.'

'It's not like the Kailya, is it?' asked Jock.

'No.' The Aye-aye drew the word out. 'Only water—harmless water.' He smiled slightly. 'But don't fall in.'

They started to move again. The cold mist rose high above them in a slow-moving canopy that blocked any hint of the sun above. The whole area seemed to have been cast into an endless dusk.

As they progressed, the tracts of grass began to narrow, and in places the murky water edged its way up onto the land. Their strange guide turned to face them. 'Very dangerous this next part,' he said, eyeing each of them in turn. 'Step only where I step.' For the next half-hour, they tramped through the marsh in single file behind the Aye-aye, who tested each step before taking another.

Jock shivered and tried to take his mind off the eeriness of the place. He thought of his home; he was only some sixty miles away from it, but it felt so much further. As he stared ahead, the pale mists before him suddenly evoked a particular memory.

On heavy late winter days the waters off the coast of Bedlington were sometimes blanketed by thick fog. Blown in by the winds, it settled over the small town, shrouding it in white. The Cleggis Point lighthouse, which spent most of the year deserted, shone its beams out over the sea and all manner of bells rang through the fog as ships large and small signalled their presence to the shore.

As the winter months approached Jock recalled these sounds and looked forward to them; waking to the bells, wandering down to the promenade in a thick warm coat and drinking milky tea in the Ice Wolf, where he would watch through the windows as the ships loomed up slowly out of the fog.

He was wrenched away from this reverie by a sharp rippling sound off to his left and spun around quickly.

'That was no marsh gas,' he said tensely. 'There's something out there.'

'I know. Where's the Aye-aye?' Aramis said. The two friends turned about to see, but the creature had vanished.

'I don't like this,' Jock muttered. 'Where've you got to, lad?' he cried out, struggling to keep his voice calm and friendly. There was a sudden grotesque cackle from the Aye-aye.

'Oh you don't need a guide now. Not anymore,' he said. Jock and Aramis looked into the fog, but the Aye-aye had become just a voice. 'I *told* you,' he added in mock sorrow, 'there's good eating here. And I *do* like to do the right thing, so someone's getting *beetles*. But it's not me.'

His shrill laugh faded into the distance.

They heard something moving swiftly through the water. Something large, much closer than before.

Aramis was dimly aware of a presence around him, and of Jock's voice, strained and fearful, calling out a warning. Suddenly a cold wet arm locked around Aramis's throat. Instinctively, he wrapped both of his paws about it, and struggling for breath, tore himself

free. He spun round and his eyes widened as he saw
what had attacked him: tall and skeletal almost to the
point of emaciation. Its gaunt limbs were covered in
glittering grey scales and a long tail snaked away behind
it under the water.

The creature let out a high-pitched shriek and
lunged at Aramis, its outstretched arms grasping
hungrily. Aramis stared up at the head that jutted out
monstrously at him, its eyes nothing more than tiny
hooded slits in the bloodless face. Its enormous leech
mouth opened, revealing countless layers of gnashing
teeth, dripping with putrid marsh water.

As Aramis backed away, Jock tore his pack from his
shoulders and searched frantically for something to use
as a weapon. Seizing the only thing he thought might
help, he dragged out a solid brass lantern and flung it
as hard as he could. It struck the creature's back and
left a welt on its glistening hide. Thick black blood
seeped from the wound and with a roar the thing
turned its eyes on Jock. It gave a single piercing screech
as its tail swept suddenly out of the water, slammed into
him and sent him staggering backwards into the mud.

Then it turned on Aramis, sprang forward and
grabbed hold of his jacket, tearing him from the ground
and snatching him up to its open mouth. He could see

down the dark throat, past the churning teeth, and feel its rank breath hot on his face. He struggled to free himself, but was held fast by its powerful claws.

Suddenly the creature froze, raised its head and stood motionless. Whatever it sensed filled its cry with fear. It dropped Aramis to the ground, turned and leapt into the murky waters of the marsh and vanished.

Jock staggered to his feet and stumbled over to his friend. 'Are you all right, lad?' he said as he helped him up.

Aramis nodded weakly. 'What was that?' he gasped as he wiped the mud from his face. 'Why did it let me go?'

'I don't know,' said Jock. 'But something frightened it just now.'

'What could such a thing possibly fear?'

'*That!*' Jock pointed to the scarlet eyes glowing in the fog.

CHAPTER NINE

The others

Elsewhere on the Wain, Philios Charon cursed softly to himself as he fought through a cluster of thorny bushes. He shook his head and pulled his hat down tightly over his ears. He was without his cane but had an ornate scabbard belted to his waist and from it he drew a long silver knife and began to hack away at the branches. Behind him strode Baron Taras and, a little further behind, Lady Nefertiti.

Philios thought back on the day's events and scowled. Not long after they came ashore they had encountered some wretched native of the place, which the Baron had identified as an Aye-aye. Philios disliked it immediately and the feeling only intensified when he

was required to hunt for the beetles the Aye-aye
demanded for guiding them across the land. But he had
to admit the strange creature had served them well
enough—until recently. All morning he had led them
on, circling around the vast swampland, dipping into
the bag for a beetle and glancing back at his charges as
though he was afraid they would try to take his prize
back from him.

Making their way through a dark forest, they had
sometimes heard the scuttling of unseen creatures, but
the journey had been without incident. Then the land
sloped sharply upwards and the trees thinned out,
giving way to a vague path littered with huge boulders
and crowded by dense scrub. From this point their
guide had started to behave oddly. His pace had slowed
and he had appeared increasingly reluctant to go on
until he simply refused.

'All right, then,' the gibbon had snapped, 'I'll be
having that bag back.'

At this the Aye-aye had snarled viciously and dashed
off into the scrub with a hiss.

Philios had started after him, but the Baron said,
'No, leave it—we have no more need of him.'

Returning to the bear's side, Philios muttered, 'The
lazy little fiend!'

'Don't be a dolt, Philios,' Lady Nefertiti had replied unexpectedly. 'It was not laziness. Clearly he was terrified of something.'

Taras had given a short nod. 'Indeed he was.'

So now that there were just the three of them once again, they pushed on.

'How do we know this is the right way?' Philios said, hacking fiercely at a low-hanging branch. 'Or even that this city exists? That little imp was most likely lying through his teeth.'

'It exists,' the Baron replied firmly. 'And furthermore, it is near.'

Lady Nefertiti appeared as relaxed as ever, moving with an easy, elegant stride. She was nonetheless highly attuned to the environment around her and had been ever since they set foot upon the Wain. There was little that escaped her attention and she usually spotted danger long before anyone else. After the Aye-aye ran off, a shadow started to form in her mind: there was something about this place that she could not quite gauge and it was making her anxious.

They had not gone much further when she came to an abrupt halt. She raised her head and sniffed several times at the air. 'Wait!' she called suddenly. Philios and the Baron stopped.

'What is it, my Lady?' the Baron said softly.

'I'm not sure,' she said. She stepped past her companions and, narrowing her eyes, stared closely at the ground. On the trail ahead she could see almost imperceptible clouds of dust rising into the air, as though in response to the footfalls of some large approaching creature. But her senses told her that no such creature was near.

'I don't see anything,' Philios Charon said, shifting his feet.

'There *is* something,' she said.

Very slowly she bent down, placed her ear near the ground and pressed her paw flat against the earth as she did so. Yes. She could feel it now. There was a creature approaching, but it was not *on* the path. 'Get back!' she cried, and at the same time there came a deep rumble as the earth immediately before her was flung aside, scattering soil and small pebbles in every direction.

Writhing its way up from a hole in the ground was an enormous bloated maggot. Its heavy white bulk twitched and rippled as it emerged fully, its body close to five feet in length. It slid across the ground towards

Nefertiti, its sharp jaws snapping with a single-minded hunger.

Philios Charon jumped back. The Baron stood his ground, but raised a paw and wrapped it around the hilt of his dagger. He did not draw the weapon; simply waited, watching Lady Nefertiti.

As soon as the creature appeared the cat had unsheathed her claws. They were as sharp as any blade and exceptionally long. She stood unmoving; her eyes locked on the creature as it glided across the earth with surprising swiftness. It lunged with its mouth wide open.

In a motion so fluid that it appeared a single gesture, she rolled out of its path, leapt to her feet and drove a single claw deep into the back of its neck.

With a low moan, the thing gave a shudder and slumped motionless.

Lady Nefertiti stood quite still for a moment, then with a snap of her wrist she raised her arm and retracted her claws with a flourish. She turned to her companions.

'Nice of you to lend a hand, my dear Charon,' she said wryly.

'I would've jumped in—if it had killed you,' Philios replied coldly.

'Oh undoubtedly,' she said, her green eyes glittering. 'You know, it's a shame you haven't brought along your customary whacking stick, Philios. We might still come across another ancient sloth you could threaten.'

'Shut your trap!' he snarled. She smiled sweetly, then turned to the Baron. 'Well, at least now we know what had the Aye-aye so frightened.'

The Baron pressed his lips together. 'No,' he said, 'this was not what he feared—not if I judged him rightly. Aye-ayes are not overly given to fear, my Lady. They are curious by nature. And while our guide's habits were far from the finest I have encountered, he was not dull-witted. This is, after all, his home. He knows the ways of the creatures that lurk about the Wain. No, something else caused him to flee from here. Something we shall encounter shortly, I believe.'

He stepped over the body of the creature and they pressed on. Further up the slope, they walked in silence for some time, a chill wind gusting about their ears. Gradually the trail became steeper, and for the next mile they travelled with their heads lowered, shielding their eyes from the grit borne on the air.

Finally they came to a crest and the Baron halted and stared ahead as Philios and Nefertiti caught up with him.

In front of them, the land dropped sharply away into a deep chasm, some sixty feet wide. Stretched across this was a straight narrow bridge constructed of a dark wood that seemed quite untouched by the elements. Beyond this, in the distance, were the jagged outlines of a mountain top. Philios went right to the edge and peered down. 'There's a nasty river down there,' he said, 'but it's a devilish long drop.'

The three animals headed for the bridge, but stopped when they got to it.

'Well, I guess that grubby little Aye-aye wasn't lying after all,' the gibbon said. 'Let's get going.'

The Baron thrust an arm across his chest. 'Wait!' he commanded. 'Remember where you are, Philios, my friend,' he said as he lowered his arm. 'All is not as it appears to be.'

He stood for a moment, his brow furrowed and his paw resting against his chin, then he flicked open his cloak. Attached to his belt was an assortment of cloth pouches. He reached into one and withdrew a tiny embroidered bag tied with a golden drawstring. He opened it and took from it a pinch of fine blue dust.

Closing his eyes, he drew in a deep breath and made a series of precise, fluid gestures, as though he were tracing symbols in the air before him, all the while murmuring in an unfamiliar, but darkly melodic language. Suddenly he opened his eyes wide and, speaking a final curt phrase, flung the pinch of dust up into the air.

Lady Nefertiti stared in astonishment as the dust, rather than fall to the ground, hung motionless in front of his head. It appeared as though the passage of time had been halted for the dust alone. He barely raised his paw and at once the motes of dust began to glitter and twinkle like tiny bursts of azure fire.

'So it is true?' Nefertiti whispered in awe. 'Philios's talk of sorcery was not as idle as I believed.'

The gibbon glanced swiftly at her. 'What did you expect?' he said scornfully. 'Perhaps you owe me an apology, dear Lady.'

'Perhaps I do,' the cat replied, her eyes never shifting from the Baron, 'but I should not expect one, were I you. So, tell me, Baron,' she purred, 'how is this possible? How do you bring these legends about you to life?'

It seemed as though the Baron had not heard her. He stared through the suspended dust motes to the bridge beyond. To the others, the structure was unaltered, but to his eyes alone, the image of the bridge seemed to shift, and he began to perceive powerful runes laid into the wood by its makers. Suddenly he understood the magic that would be set in motion were he to walk across this bridge unprepared.

Nefertiti's words echoed softly. *How was it possible?* The Baron smiled. Powdered lapis lazuli mixed with the crushed leaves of the hirrallia plant. The right symbols, each one exact and precise, and then of course, the incantation itself. That was his discovery. A rediscovery of an ancient art, admittedly, but his nonetheless. Decades of work, all told, but the nature of the glamour was revealed to him.

'Ingenious,' he whispered. 'The Aye-aye was right to fear this.' He gazed for a moment longer, then closed his paw tightly. The dust before him blazed with greater intensity and was consumed in blue flame.

He turned to Philios and Nefertiti. 'Now we must cross. Stay close to me.' And so saying he began the casting of the charm that would allow them to pass safely over the bridge.

CHAPTER TEN

The Alession

Jock and Aramis edged slowly backwards through the murky waters of the marsh.

'There are more!' Jock hissed, as all around they saw many pairs of red eyes fixed on them. Shifting forms, like furtive visions in the gloom, kept circling them, so that whichever way they turned they were aware of shapes moving towards them through the mist: a frightening band of creatures, in size and shape like great white wolves. But as the figures drew nearer, Jock and Aramis saw that a spectral translucence clung to their gaunt frames.

'*Ghost Wolves*,' said Jock in a thin voice.

As the words left his lips, the largest of the creatures stepped forth. He came close to Jock and Aramis and tilted his pale head slightly, his eyes glistening in the half-light. '*Ghost Wolves?*' he echoed with dark bemusement. 'Yes, that is what they call us in the outer lands. But we do not go by that name here.'

Jock and Aramis looked about them. Their path forward was completely blocked by the wolf's powerful body and as they spun around seeking escape, another fear came upon them—that the beast from the water might reappear.

The great wolf drew even nearer. 'That creature— the Caleesh—will not return,' he said, 'for it fears us. Nevertheless, it is unwise for *you* to remain in the marshes. There are *other* things—worse things—in this place. Come,' he said firmly.

Jock stayed close to Aramis. 'What could be *worse* than this?' he whispered. 'We must get away.'

'And where would you run to?' the wolf said suddenly. All the two friends could see were eyes closing in on them from every side as more wolves appeared in the fog.

'I see dread in your eyes,' said the wolf, 'and given what we are, that is to be expected. I am Feldar of the Alessian Wolves. Fear me, but do not mistrust me.'

He padded softly away from them and Jock and Aramis fell in behind him.

The ring of wolves loped almost without sound through the marsh as Jock and Aramis stumbled to keep up with them. Aramis moved awkwardly, the pain from the Caleesh's attack now seeping through his body. His paw strayed to the side of his neck where the blood had broken through the fur. Beside him, Jock trotted stiffly, his face tense, his eyes constantly searching for an opportunity to break free. The chill waters of the marsh splashed against their legs, and coated them with thick dark mud.

After they had travelled a little way, the land began to rise slightly and they felt dry, firm earth once again under their feet. Feldar drew to a halt, and as Jock and Aramis staggered up behind him they saw a great shape, like a wall of shadow, looming out of the mist ahead. They had come to the edge of a dark forest.

Tall black trees rose up before them, at first reminding the two friends of the majestic tapen forests to the north of Ravenwood. But these trees did not possess the rich natural colour of the tapens—it was as though the blackness had been inflicted upon them, as if some mineral, drawn up from the earth had passed into their veins, infusing them with a poison they had tried to expel through their bark.

As Jock and Aramis stared warily into the dim forest, Feldar turned to them. 'You should not wander recklessly in these lands,' he said gravely. 'And I should be more cautious in my choice of guide if I were you. The Aye-ayes are not greatly blessed with integrity. It was fortunate that only one Caleesh heard you moving about in the marsh.'

'Only one?' said Jock.

The wolf nodded. 'There are older and larger Caleeshes dwelling in those waters,' he said dryly. 'Had you met one of them, you would now be dead.'

'We have you to thank, then, that we are not,' said Jock, still eyeing the wolf suspiciously.

'We did not enter the marsh to save you,' Feldar said. 'It was but fortune that our way took us there.' He shifted slightly. 'I wonder what it is that brings you to this place,' he continued. 'Unarmed and with little care for your own lives.'

'We are following another group of creatures,' said Aramis.

Feldar stared at the two friends and in his eyes they saw a glimmer of recognition. 'We have seen them,' he said, 'a group of three. One bears the Crest of Symara and that is most curious, as we have not seen that symbol for many years.'

At the mention of the Crest, Aramis shot him a look. 'We *must* find these travellers,' he said. 'Can you tell us which direction they were heading?'

'They are journeying to Kryl-Gavesk, ancient city of the Elmasen,' said Feldar. 'We watched them, though we ourselves chose to remain unseen. Their path is of little interest to us.'

'But it is greatly important to *us*,' said Jock. 'They mean to enter the city and seek something that may still lie within.'

'That city is desolate,' said Feldar. 'Whatever power once dwelt there is long past. What do we care for those who wish to wander its shattered floors?' He turned away from them. 'The day wanes,' he said. 'You would do well to seek shelter before nightfall. We shall part here.' Signalling mutely to his companions, he began to move off.

As he did so, Aramis called to him. 'The bear does not come idly. He carries the Binding Stone of the Elmasen.'

At these words Feldar halted. He stared at Aramis. 'I do not think that likely,' he said.

'It is true,' replied Aramis.

'The Stone disappeared many centuries ago,' said Feldar.

'The Stone was found.'

Feldar's face grew grave. He glanced at the wolves behind him and mused. 'Perhaps Lord Varios should hear of this.' Turning again to Jock and Aramis, he said, 'Come with us, then—and stay close.' He moved off briskly into the forest, a sinister grace clinging to his slender frame as he padded deftly over the branches and stones that lay across his path. Aramis and Jock followed uneasily.

As they travelled deeper into the forest the fog began to disperse. Although there was no hint of wind they could hear the thick leaves rustling like countless pairs of tiny hands rubbing dryly together.

Around them the trees grew into ever more grotesque and disturbing shapes, entwining about each other and casting deep shadows on the forest floor. In places the roots had broken through the ground and lay tangled across the path like coiled snakes, and Jock and Aramis had to move slowly and cautiously to avoid stumbling.

After they had journeyed for several miles the forest around them became sparser and in the distance there rose two immense stone sculptures of great wolves crouched in readiness, their surfaces splintered and cracked as if untended for centuries. Passing between these, they came to a wide clearing, flanked on three sides by steep rock walls. Two of these surfaces bore low, dark openings—cave entrances perhaps. The area formed a kind of natural amphitheatre, well shielded from winds or the stealthy approach of unwanted visitors. Around its perimeter stood a curving line of roughly hewn stone pillars, weathered and stained with bands of mottled ebony moss.

In the centre of this clearing sat a huge wolf, the pallid whiteness of his gaunt form broken only by a thin strip of faded grey fur that ran in an uneven line down the length of his back. His steady eyes fixed upon the troupe as they entered the arena.

'Lord Varios,' said Feldar as he approached the solitary figure, 'I bring news.' Jock and Aramis watched as the two creatures spoke in hushed words together, but they could make out nothing of what was being said. They grew uneasy when both wolves turned in their direction, their scarlet eyes gleaming like fragments of dark ruby. Finally Varios gave a slow nod, and as Feldar stepped aside, Jock and Aramis found themselves standing directly before the sharp gaze of this imposing creature.

He studied them silently. 'We do not see many travellers on The Wain,' he said at last in a voice with a rich and timeless resonance. 'In fact, years often pass between sightings—many years.'

As he spoke there was a movement behind Jock and Aramis, and a long procession of wolves began to emerge from the cave entrances. All bore the same ethereal translucence, their paws leaving no trace as they padded across the dry dust of the clearing.

'You come with strange tidings of the return of the Binding Stone,' said Varios. 'Tell me what you know.' As Jock and Aramis moved closer to him, some of the pale creatures around the perimeter dropped to their haunches; others stood motionless, with stern expressions fixed on their faces.

Aramis began to recount in a halting voice his chance discovery of the Stone and all that had since befallen him. When he had finished the great wolf nodded.

'And what is it you propose now?' he said.

'We wish to stop those who have taken it. We were told that the Stone is one half of a larger artefact. If the Baron finds the other half he will wield a terrible power.'

'Indeed he will,' said Varios. 'He will join the two and summon the Bora.'

As this last word was spoken a chill wind swept right through the clearing.

'The Bora?' said Jock fearfully. 'That is the creature trapped in the Stone?'

For an instant the wolf's brows drew tightly together. 'Not a *creature* as you would know it,' he said. 'The Bora is a dark demon with no place in this world. It was called forth from a shadow realm by the Elmasen.'

'Who would wish to do such a thing?' asked Jock.

Varios looked at him. 'One who desired power beyond all else. Such a one governed the Elmasen. Cadell was his name, the elder of two brothers. He was a wise leader, greatly skilled in the arts of Magic. But during the long years of his reign he became possessed of a growing ambition. Less was he seen walking among his people. For many days and nights he cloistered himself in his chamber until at last he had fashioned the Binding Stone and set it atop a silver staff. It was an extraordinary feat of Magic—extraordinary, but perilous, for the Stone was created for one purpose: to trap a spirit of darkness.

'Soon afterwards he summoned forth the Bora, imprisoning the creature within the very substance of the rock. With such a powerful being at his command, he believed the Elmasen would be invincible. His followers revered him, but in the heart of his brother, Kharek, a venomous envy was growing. He sought power and leadership for himself and watched bitterly as Cadell grew ever more honoured among his race.

'Driven by his savage craving, Kharek seized the staff, called forth the Bora from its stony prison and set it upon his own people. It wreaked a terrible havoc on the city and its inhabitants while the two brothers fought a deadly battle for possession of the staff. Cadell managed to wrest it back and commanded the Bora to return to the Stone. As the creature did so, Kharek made a desperate lunge for the Binding Stone, wrenched it from the crown of the staff and escaped with it.

'But he was gravely wounded and, though he fled from these parts, it was clear he would not survive the injuries he bore for long. By the end of that struggle, most of the Elmasen had been slain. The survivors lay for some days about the steps of their city, until they too were claimed by death.

'Thus came the end of the great cats and their civilisation and with it came the disappearance of the Binding Stone.' Varios paused. 'It is clear,' he said, turning to Aramis, 'that Kharek must have made his way north from the Wain. And in some far place both his life and this Stone were lost.'

'Then centuries later a farmer found it and took it to my grandfather,' said Aramis.

'So it would seem.'

'But how did you learn of all that happened to the Elmasen?' asked Jock suddenly.

'I did not learn. I was there,' said Varios.

'You were there? But I don't understand. How is that possible?' said Jock.

The wolf shifted slightly, his eyes upon the distant trees. 'We, the Alessian, are not like your kind. We are, as you would understand the word, *immortal*.'

Above them the daylight was growing fainter, all the shadows lengthening in dark pools across the ground.

'Immortal?' echoed Jock.

'We do not live forever, but our life spans are so great that to you we would seem eternal. We have seen ages rise and fall.'

'Are you sorcerers—like the Elmasen?' asked Jock.

'No,' said Varios. 'It is not magic—it is our nature. You call us Ghost Wolves. We are not ghosts; nor are we quite flesh and blood. We live apart from others, with one paw in the spirit world, you might say.'

'*Spirit creatures*,' whispered Jock. 'This is indeed a day of strange revelations. Not even the most fanciful of sailors would have guessed the truth.'

Aramis reflected. What he had heard of the Ghost Wolves astonished him. It was as if a new world were opening up—one far removed from all he had ever known. The past that he had only explored on stones and in scrolls lay before him now in the ageless face of the great wolf. Were it not for the urgency of his quest, he could have sat for many hours before the pale creature. There was much he wished to ask, but his thoughts kept returning to the Bora. *A dark demon from a shadow realm*, Varios had called it. And this was what the Baron carried as he headed for Kryl-Gavesk.

Aramis looked up at last. 'You were there during the time of the great Elmasen battle,' he said to Varios. 'Do you know what became of the controlling staff?'

'It remained in the city,' said Varios, 'in the dead grip of its maker.'

'And this Bora has been trapped in the Stone all these centuries?' said Jock.

'Trapped and filled with hate,' said Varios. 'This is not its world—it belongs nowhere here.'

'No,' said Aramis. 'It clearly does not. And the Baron cannot be allowed to master such a thing. We *must* follow him.' He looked anxiously at Varios. 'Can you help us?'

'The Alessian do not involve themselves greatly in the lives of mortals,' said Varios. 'That you have been brought among us this day is most uncommon.' In the waning light the wolves around them appeared more insubstantial than ever, their forms merging with the rock walls behind them.

Jock spoke to the circle of wolves. 'You are immortal and so this Bora is perhaps of little matter to you,' he said. 'But to us, to the world *we* live in, it would bring horror and destruction. We don't view our lives as insignificant, even if they seem brief to your eyes. Where we have come from there is much that makes life worthwhile—much that I wish to protect.'

As he spoke, Feldar suddenly rose on all fours. 'Lord Varios,' he said, 'I think perhaps this is some mortal business in which we ought to be involved.' He looked for a moment at Jock and Aramis. 'I will lead them to Kryl-Gavesk,' he said. 'I have listened to their words. They are unlike the Aye-ayes in their speech and unlike most creatures we have encountered in our long lives.' He paused. 'I will take them as far as the city.'

Varios nodded. 'If you choose to do this, then you should go swiftly, Feldar. Evening draws on and they will not find the journey an easy one.'

Feldar turned to Jock and Aramis. 'Prepare yourselves,' he said.

The two friends tightened the straps on their shoulders and then looked at Feldar. They were ready.

Varios looked down at them. 'May fortune favour you,' he said solemnly. He turned to Feldar, who stood patiently to one side. 'Go quickly,' he said.

Feldar nodded once and sprang silently from the clearing. After a final glance at Varios, Jock and Aramis hurried after him.

CHAPTER ELEVEN

The Bridge

They passed for a second time under the great statues and Feldar took a sharp turn north-west, leading them back through the dark trees of the forest. He moved at a swift trot, checking from time to time to see that Jock and Aramis had not dropped behind. Sometimes he would urge them on with a brief word, but for the most part their journey was in silence; the two friends struggling to keep up with their guide.

They travelled through the shadows cast by the heavy trees, the long sagging branches twisting about their shoulders, and the air around them growing ever more still and lifeless.

As their path began to veer more sharply to the north, the undergrowth thickened and forced them to leap awkwardly over thorny shrubs while stooping under the overhead tangle of branches that clawed fiercely at their clothing. Feldar occasionally paused to observe their plight, his lithe spectral form untouched by the hostility of the forest.

They had covered almost three miles when the sky became visible more frequently through the thinning trees. At last they had reached the northern edge of the forest.

'Stay close to me,' Feldar whispered. 'There is a chasm ahead that we must cross to reach the city.'

Jock and Aramis were weary, but Feldar pushed off again, his muzzle close to the ground. 'The others have passed this way,' he said, 'and they have left the smell of death behind them.' He continued cautiously now, skirting around a cluster of boulders that obscured the way ahead. A little distance beyond these they came upon the lifeless form of the creature Nefertiti had slain.

Feldar walked slowly towards it. 'It was a swift kill,' he said as he gazed at the beast.

'Aye, well the Baron is strong,' said Jock.

Feldar shook his head. 'It was not he, but the dark cat who travels with him. She has done this.' He sniffed at the air and then leapt across the starkly outstretched body.

Jock and Aramis edged nervously around the creature and followed Feldar past the shattered ground where the thing had broken through the earth. Ahead of them the path grew steeper and they could hear a deep sound as of wind echoing through a long tunnel.

'What is that?' asked Aramis.

'Our crossing,' Feldar called back to him. 'Come.'

They climbed a little further, then the wolf drew to a halt and Jock and Aramis came up beside him. Before them all, the land levelled for a short way before dropping into a sheer chasm, at the bottom of which flowed a swirling river. The deep roar of swiftly moving water was lifted on the wind, as if the river itself was calling to them in broken wails.

Stretched out across the chasm was a long, narrow bridge. 'The Elmasen made this,' said Feldar as he led them to its edge. 'You must cross it quickly. Keep your thoughts focused on other things. This bridge has its own voice,' he added gravely, 'and it may whisper strange tidings to the minds of mortals. I shall go first,' he said.

He stepped lightly onto the bridge. Aramis watched his agile movements, then leant over to Jock. 'Come on,' he said.

The two friends strode rapidly across the narrow bridge in single file, with Aramis leading. Their footfalls seemed oddly deadened, as if the natural sound of their passing was being swallowed up by the bridge itself, and something about its design made both animals uncomfortable. Glancing down, Aramis thought he could see strange markings in the ancient timbers, but it seemed that time had made them very faint. He hurried across and was relieved to feel the hard rock underfoot once again.

'That was an eerie sensation, wasn't it?' he called out over his shoulder. Jock did not answer and when Aramis turned, there was his friend still standing in the middle of the bridge. His head was cocked to one side and his eyes narrowed as though he was straining to hear something. 'Do not tarry,' said Feldar, as he stood beside Aramis. Jock shook his head slightly and a strange look came into his eyes. He had something important to do—something—he couldn't remember exactly what. 'Don't worry—there's nothing wrong here,' he said dreamily. 'Nothing at all.'

'He must not stay there,' said Feldar urgently.

'Jock, come on. It's dangerous!' Aramis yelled.

Jock stood motionless, his eyes closed. Aramis was calling to him, but his voice was far away and besides they could afford to take a wee break now, surely. They had been walking forever. He smiled. It was so quiet here. The air was still: heavy, sweet-scented, but not oppressive, and there was a hush about the place that was thick and beautiful. It was as though a vast bell had been struck long ago, and he felt that if he held his breath and listened he could just hear its final dying call.

And then the wind began to blow. It was almost imperceptible at first, nothing more than a slight stirring, the air about him moving a fraction. It was becoming colder too, or so it seemed. The difference in temperature was so slight that it was hard to be sure. Jock opened his eyes and looked at Aramis and Feldar standing there at the end of the bridge. There was something about them—a strange alteration, something small and difficult to define. Staring at Feldar, he could have sworn that the translucence of the wolf's fur had been clearer before. Now he appeared more shadow-wolf than ghost. It had to be a trick of the light. Rubbing his eyes, he looked at him again. No, it was no trick. Feldar's colour had changed in some subtle way and, beyond that, his expression seemed to have become harder, more severe. Beside him Aramis was looking very tired, as though he had not slept in days. His eyes were bloodshot and his face was haggard and grim. And, it seemed, thinner.

The thought came to him that he should get off this bridge, leave immediately. And he would have done so but for that far off sound—the peal of the great bell. The wind was more insistent now—a current moving, swelling, sighing. And in that distant ringing a voice seemed to be carried. Was it borne on the wind? No, no. Somehow it was buried deep inside the bell, or perhaps it *was* the bell, tolling centuries ago. If he could just understand the voice. Closing his eyes again, he strained to listen.

When he opened them, he had no idea how much time had passed. A second? A minute? Hours, maybe. His glazed eyes tried to take in his surroundings. The colour had gone from everything: the rock, the sky, the hues of the forest had been replaced by dead shades of grey and black and white, and he could hear nothing but the ringing in his ears.

He shivered. The air was colder now that the wind had picked up. As it swept around him it seemed to pull at his fur, reaching into him and caressing the skin underneath with sharp probing fingers. They were clutching at him, trying to find a way in. Through flesh and bone, through sinew, through heart, digging into his soul. What was wrong with his friends? Didn't they feel it, this evil? Could they not hear the voice? How could they be unaware of it? He looked at them and his eyes grew wide with horror. The two figures waiting across the bridge were not his friends! They were monstrous. Where Feldar had been there now swayed a repulsive travesty of the white wolf, its grinning head lolling at an impossible angle on its scrawny neck, its crooked jaws hanging agape. Jock tried to swallow, but could not. The wolf-thing laughed, its icy voice distant and, loathsome as it was to behold, far worse was the creature standing next to it. The breath fled from Jock's lungs.

He was staring at a quivering, lurching corpse, cracked and splintered bones protruding from its dead flesh. Its head was bulbous, misshapen. Its hollow eye-sockets fixed on him, it cackled grotesquely.

Jock was terrified. He *had* to get off the bridge. He placed one paw on the rail and stood there frozen. The black whisperings urged him; the bell and the wind now indistinguishable. Grinding his teeth, he fought to block out the sounds. For a fraction of a second there was silence and clarity, and in that moment he understood the nature of his peril. Letting go of the rail, he moved forward. He had not taken two steps before he was overwhelmed by the terrible screaming, whispering, pealing in a single savage crescendo.

The wind tore at him, ripped and stung him with its words of madness. He tried to block the sound with one paw and fell to his knees, struggling to drag himself forward with the other. There was a scratching, grating sound under the howling. He looked up. The dead thing was coming for him. He could see it hefting its deformed body, and the sight was too much for him. He collapsed to the ground, clamping both paws over his ears.

A chalky bone encircled his waist. The feel of it against his fur was sickening. It was pulling him, dragging him to the wolf-creature. He knew now that the other thing had him and would never let go. He squeezed his eyes tightly shut and felt himself dragged once again.

Suddenly the wind and the bell and the insane whisperings had gone. The thing was not holding him anymore. Jock opened his eyes and found himself cradled by Aramis. On his friend's face was a look of deep concern.

'Jock! Can you hear me?' Aramis was saying, his voice soft and soothing.

'Laddie,' Jock sobbed, coughing. 'It's you! It's you!' He sat up slowly and looked around. The colour had returned to the forest; the creatures were no longer there. Perhaps they never had been. He had fallen down and Aramis had come to get him. Then that dead *thing* was—no, he could not bear to dwell on it! He shuddered thinking how close he had come to throwing himself from the high deck of the bridge.

Aramis looked at his friend. 'It's over,' he said gently. 'Whatever happened to you out there is finished.'

'Ah,' Jock said, taking a deep breath, 'the things I saw! You'd thank me if I never spoke of them. I saw you and Feldar, but you were—no! I won't talk about it. It was horrible.'

Aramis nodded once and moved to stand up, but Jock placed a paw upon his arm and said, 'Thank you, laddie. Thank you.'

'It was nothing, my friend.' Aramis smiled.

'How long was I out there?' asked Jock as he rose shakily to his feet.

'Only a moment.'

'A moment was it?' Jock said vaguely.

Feldar watched them keenly as they spoke, his eyes shifting between the two of them and the bridge. They seemed suddenly aware of his presence.

'So that was Elmasen hospitality.' Jock shivered.

Feldar stared past him at the shadowy contours of the bridge. 'It was a defence,' he said. 'Those unskilled in the ways of Magic have not usually fared well on this crossing.'

'Aye,' said Jock slowly. 'Aye, I'm certain they have not. How far have we to go?'

'The city is close,' said Feldar.

'Then let's be off,' said Jock.

Aramis looked at him. 'Are you quite ready?' he asked.

'Aye, lad,' said Jock. 'I am.'

Feldar nodded and on they went.

They passed through a barren stretch of earth where little grew but tall, coarse grasses. Beyond this, the land dropped away again into the slopes of a deep, treeless valley. On its farthest side, silhouetted against the backdrop of a pale mountain wall, stood the ancient city of Kryl-Gavesk.

CHAPTER TWELVE

Kryl-Gavesk

It rose starkly from the valley floor, a series of ornate buildings crowned at either end by spiralling turrets, the upper crests of which were threaded with deep veins of jade and silver. Across the roof lay thousands of intricate mosaics, each tile covered with a fine glaze that glistened as if still damp.

But for a central archway, the entire city was enclosed by high walls of stone.

Jock and Aramis hesitated at first.

'I will take you below now,' said Feldar, 'into the valley of the Elmasen.' He leapt forward and began descending the slope in swift strides, Aramis and Jock running apprehensively behind him.

They reached the valley floor and drew nearer to the city. The symmetry of the buildings gave a strange harmony to the scene, but within the meticulous balance and order lay a hint of discord. As the sun began to set, vivid streams of colour splashed over the roof, cloaking its towers in thick scarlet stains.

'I wish you good luck,' said the wolf. 'And I suspect you may need it.' He raised his muzzle and sniffed at the air, and then bowing his head once, quickly bounded away, his pale form like the elusive vision of a mist. Back up on the ridge, he looked one last time at the two friends and then strode into the distance.

Walking through the archway and into the city, Jock and Aramis found themselves in an open courtyard that curved in a wide arc inside the perimeter of the buildings. Directly ahead of them stood the vast central hall of Kryl-Gavesk, its walls merging with the sheer face of the mountainside behind.

On the ground before it was an octagonal pool with waters the colour of dark emerald ink in the fading light. It was fed from a jagged rent high in the wall above and a steady sheet of water cascaded sharply down the side of the building, striking at last an irregular piece of rock that lay just below the surface of the pool. The hiss from the falling waters echoed like the whispering of many voices. No other sound broke the intense desolation of this place.

They climbed a series of wide stone steps leading to one of two arched entranceways that flanked the pool.

When they reached the top they halted. Sprawled awkwardly before them lay a skeleton, the bones bleached by the sun, the distinctively feline jaw stretched open in a hideous grimace. About the creature's chest curved a suit of silver armour, the plating shredded as if huge claws had torn effortlessly through the metal. Beside the skeleton lay a weathered scabbard with the sword still in it. Jock bent down to pull the sword free and it came forth awkwardly, the blade dull and rusted.

'Poor fellow never even had time to draw it,' said Jock as he studied the long blade. 'It would have been a fine weapon once.' He laid it down carefully.

As they continued towards the entrance, he turned once to look back at the skeleton. As he did so he saw for the first time that the stone submerged in the pool was in fact the sculpted head of an enormous cat. Its two dull eyes stared up blankly from the shallow waters as the ceaseless torrent fell on its weathered features. 'It must have tumbled from above,' he muttered.

Then he and Aramis passed into the great hall.

Most of the faint light in this vast curving chamber came from swirling bands of pale phosphorescent stone inlaid in the ceiling. 'Lilasium,' Jock said wistfully. 'Probably mined in the far north.'

Round the circumference of the room ran a circle of columns, the wide base of each pillar fashioned into the shape of an outstretched paw. Many of these bore deep scorch marks while others were scored by long cuts, as though enormous blades had hewn viciously into the rock.

As the friends' eyes adjusted to the light, they could make out the ivory shapes of skeletons scattered across the floor. Most lay in awkward positions that spoke of an anguished struggle to escape. The claws of some still gripped at the heels of others as if they had fallen together and then crawled forward in their last desperate moments.

Aramis bent down to examine the floor. There were fresh tracks on the crumbled stone where the others had passed through, their trail leading to a dark opening at the far end of the room. He stood up. 'Come on,' he said.

They crossed the room and entered a long shadowy corridor that appeared to have been cut through solid rock. Like the entrance chamber, the roof was veined with lilasium, which cast a soft, pale light over everything. As they walked on they became aware of an increasing coldness that oozed from the walls.

'I believe we're passing into the side of the mountain,' said Aramis.

'Aye, so it would seem,' said Jock as he tried to rub some warmth into his arms and stared into the gloom ahead.

When they at last came to the end of the corridor they passed under an elaborately carved arch and out into another circular room. Sweeping around the walls was a large mural.

The painting portrayed the grandeur of the Elmasen civilisation and depicted the city as it had once been. Beneath high columns stood a gathering of tall cats, their fur a rich russet, their ears long and pointed like those of the lynx. They were draped in dark cloaks, each bearing the crest of Symara woven with shimmering bronze and copper thread.

Passing before the watching eyes of these robed cats was a great army of Elmasen clad in silver armour, their sharp claws glittering as they marched in step, with long spears held upright in their slender paws.

Jock and Aramis stared at the painting for a moment and then Aramis gestured ahead and they made for a passage that lay directly before them.

They had not gone far along it when they heard a faint sound coming from somewhere further on. Stopping for a minute, they listened. A low voice rose and fell about their ears.

'The Baron,' whispered Aramis.

They inched forward, ensuring that they made no sound on the smooth rock floor. The passage brought them to the base of another flight of stone steps. They climbed these with care and found themselves at the entrance to a long room, its floor made of white marble.

At the far end was an imposing high door constructed of broad planks of timber. Upon this, in orange and red, was the image of a claw grasping a full moon. It appeared as though it had been branded there, scorched by a fire that had not blackened, but rather had left the imprint of its own vivid flames.

On either side of the door was a recessed alcove containing a small pedestal. The one on the left was empty, but in the other stood a tall metal statue of an armoured Elmasen, a long spear clasped tightly in its paws.

And there, in the centre of the room, was the Baron, his attention fixed on the door. At his side stood Philios Charon and Lady Nefertiti.

'Professor Taras!' Aramis called loudly.

Philios and Nefertiti spun around immediately. At the sight of Jock and Aramis, the gibbon let out a low snarl and tightened his long fingers around the hilt of his knife. Lady Nefertiti studied the intruders calmly.

Taras himself turned when he was ready. He frowned as he beheld the pair, but nobody spoke. Jock and Aramis moved closer. Taras stared down at them. 'So, you followed me,' he began, 'across the water and across the Wain. I confess that is something I did not expect. You impress me—and as you may imagine, I am not easily impressed. To journey all this way, you must be eager for something. So tell me, what is it that I can do for you?'

'You know the answer,' replied Aramis steadily, his eyes never straying from the Baron's. 'We have come for the Stone.'

'Have you indeed?' the bear growled.

'It does not belong to you,' said Jock.

The Baron appeared to consider his next move briefly. Then he opened one of the pouches on his belt and drew forth the Stone. Turning it over slowly in his paws, he murmured to himself. 'The Binding Stone of the Elmasen.' He shot Jock and Aramis a look. 'And to whom does it belong? To you? To the late Julius Le Faye?' He touched the clasp on his throat where the symbol on the door was repeated in miniature. 'No, it is mine by right—the right of power and of magic. And force.'

'It is *yours* only because you stole it,' said Aramis defiantly.

'Is that so?' the Baron replied. 'Well then, here it is.' He held the Stone out to Aramis. 'But how will you take it from me, Le Faye?' he said, an ominous smile playing on his lips. 'Would you care to battle me for it?'

Aramis said nothing.

The bear's smile broadened a little. 'I believe you might even try,' he said. 'But as I have neither the time nor the inclination to engage in so one-sided a combat, Lady Nefertiti here will have to serve instead. Come, Philios.' And so saying he turned from his adversaries and made for the door.

Jock and Aramis stood side by side, watching as Lady Nefertiti took a step forward. Her claws remained sheathed as she studied the two of them.

Suddenly, behind her there was a startling clang of metal struck firmly on stone. She whipped around.

Climbing down from its pedestal was the figure of the Elmasen. The point of its spear now rested on the cold stone floor and as Nefertiti watched, the creature stepped forward lithely, its armoured body blocking the Baron's path to the door. It swung the spear smoothly upwards and gripped it across its chest with both paws.

The Baron and Philios fell back and the gibbon let out a savage hiss. 'One of these wretched cats is still alive!' he gasped.

'I think not,' the Baron replied evenly. 'This is some creature of sorcery—set here to guard the entrance beyond, no doubt.' He made a move and as he did, the cat raised its spear menacingly. 'Yes—it responds to my approach—still performing its task, though the race that made it passed from existence long ago.'

Jock was stunned. The statue was remarkably beautiful. Its face, formed into a stylised likeness of an Elmasen, was made of a copper coloured metal and set deep in its eye-sockets were two large garnets, pulsing with a soft red light. The creature wore the silver armour of the Elmasen cats, although the interlocking plates were more ornate in appearance, each panel finely etched with intricate geometric designs. As Jock stared at it, his keen eye caught a flash of something he thought he recognised. Unsure, he moved closer and, through a small gap between the creature's rounded shoulder plates and its embossed breastplate, he could just make out a series of slow-turning cogs.

'It's a machine!' he cried. 'A clockwork creature!'

'Clockwork?' said the Baron, glaring down at him. He reached for his dagger, but changed his mind and instead raised his paw to his face, his claws stroking the scarlet underside of his chin as he observed the guardian.

Slowly, with his eyes on the point of the guardian's spear, the Baron moved again. The creature raised its weapon once more, but this time the Baron caught hold of it. He twisted and turned the spear as he tried to wrest it away out of the creature's paw. He put all his weight against the spear, as though he sought to knock the creature to the ground or push past it, but he was powerless against the guardian's resistance.

The Baron possessed great physical strength too, but now it was his analytical skill that he called on. He had some understanding of clockwork mechanisms— enough to know that they had one great limitation. Break the right piece and they would not weaken or slow—they would simply cease functioning altogether. And so, while he was outwardly aggressive as he wrestled the creature, with his face contorted into a vicious snarl, his mind remained calm and all the while he scanned the machine, searching for its vulnerable points.

Suddenly, he was jolted back so hard that he nearly fell to the floor. But now he had the knowledge he needed. As the other animals in the room watched, he advanced on the guardian again.

Reaching out as though to seize its spear, the Baron instead drove his paw into the creature's breastplate, striking it hard in the spot where he judged the metal to be thinnest.

This appeared to have no effect, but when the bear struck a second time, in precisely the same place, the guardian let forth a low grinding sound and stumbled backwards.

The Baron aimed a third blow and this time struck the creature so hard that its breastplate buckled inward. The machine toppled over onto its back and for a moment struggled to right itself, the sharp sound of grating metal coming from within its chest. Before long, its efforts became feeble until finally, while the light from its eyes continued to glow softly, it ceased moving altogether.

Breathing heavily, the Baron simply stared at it until he was quite certain that it would not rise from the floor. Philios Charon came over to the fallen machine and sneered down at it. 'You made short work of that thing,' he said to the Baron with a sharp nod.

'Yes. And now that has been dealt with,' the Baron said, 'I believe we have wasted enough time here.' He turned to Jock and Aramis. 'Remain in this room or leave the city—do what you will, but do *not* think to follow me. My goodwill is exhausted and it will go badly for you both if I see you again.' Without looking back, he called over his shoulder, 'Come, my Lady. Mechanical cats I can deal with myself, but this city may hold other surprises.'

The cat gave Jock and Aramis a final enigmatic glance and joined the Baron.

When he reached the door, the bear thrust it open and strode through, followed swiftly by his companions. The door shut behind them with a heavy thud and Jock and Aramis heard the sound of a bolt being slid into place.

Once the footsteps of the three animals had faded away, the two friends scrambled for the door and set their shoulders hard against it, to try and shift it.

'It's no good,' said Jock. He stared at the dark timbers, where the Crest of Symara endured in its strange burnt colours. 'There's simply no way we can break through this—it's much too solid.'

Aramis cast his mind back to the path they had taken through the city. 'I don't think there's any other way around either,' he said.

'No way round it, no way through—and no way forward,' sighed Jock.

Aramis shook his head. 'That can't be the end of our options,' he said. 'We *have* to find some way to catch up with the Baron—he cannot leave here with this *Bora* under his control.' He glanced swiftly around the hall. 'What about that guardian's spear?' he said. 'We could break the door down with that.'

'I don't think so, lad,' replied Jock. 'Even with the spear it would take us all day to batter our way through.' His eyes were drawn to the guardian lying stretched out on the marble floor. An idea suddenly entered his mind—one so unlikely that he was at first doubtful whether he should mention it. He went over, knelt down beside the machine and began to examine it carefully.

'What are you doing?' asked Aramis.

'I'm not quite sure,' Jock admitted as he began tugging at the machine's twisted breastplate. 'Could you give me a hand with this?' he puffed. Aramis was puzzled, but joined in nonetheless.

The Baron's well-aimed blows had already done most of the work and with some exertion, the two friends managed to wrest the breastplate off the guardian. When they had done so, they were amazed at what they saw. There in front of them was a complex arrangement of small cogs, gears and bronze rods. Running between these were pieces of shaped glass and tiny metal hoses.

To Aramis's eyes the workings were almost entirely alien, although they did possess a cold beauty all their own.

For Jock, the mechanism was also strange, but for a different reason. He felt as though he were standing on a high mountain top, gazing down at some vast and complex maze. As he did so, almost mesmerised, he began to perceive a way through the maze to its centre. Gradually the harmony of the machine revealed itself.

He could see where the Baron's blows had damaged the workings enough to snap three small levers and push some of the springs out of alignment, but beyond that he could also see, at least in vague outline, how the creature operated.

'These brass rods attach to that glass piece up there,' he muttered, 'and then that leads up to the eyes, by the looks of things. And see there,' he pointed to a large cylinder made of brass and notched with thousands of minute filaments, 'I'm fairly certain that's its—well, its *mind*, I guess you might say.' As Jock studied the guardian's workings, for the first time since he had stepped onto the Wain, a genuine smile appeared on his face. 'I think,' he nodded, 'I think I can fix it.'

'Are you sure that would be a good thing?' asked Aramis.

'Aye,' said Jock. 'I believe I can *reset* it—almost like a clock.' He tugged at the straps of his pack, pulled it from his shoulders and began rummaging about in it. Soon he drew out a worn pouch containing a small set of tools, similar to those Aramis had noticed lying on the table in Jock's home.

'I take this little lot with me everywhere,' Jock said in response to his friend's unspoken query. 'They're my travelling tools. Never know when you might need them.'

'No, indeed!' replied Aramis. He was fascinated as Jock set to work, his paws deftly removing various parts of the guardian and reinserting them, testing the spin of the cogs and realigning springs. The process took quite a while.

'Well,' he said, 'I don't fully understand his workings—he's extraordinary, far beyond anything I could have come up with—so it's a bit of a makeshift job, but it should be enough to get him up and about again.' He grinned. 'Only one way to find out.' Reaching down, he took hold of a small dial in the centre of the guardian's chest and gave it a sharp turn. The two friends scrambled back as the guardian let out a sudden whir. For a few seconds it appeared as though Jock had failed. Then as suddenly as though it were a marionette dangling on a thread, the metal cat jerked to its feet. It stood before Jock and Aramis, its eyes glowing steadily.

'Now, easy there, laddie,' said Jock. He made some small adjustments and then began to back away. Astonished, Aramis watched as the creature followed Jock, albeit a little shakily. 'Aye, he's working!' Jock exclaimed.

'Working?' said Aramis.

'Well,' said Jock, 'I've managed to set him so that he should follow me about. And with a little luck, I think we can get him to do one or two other things, as well.'

'Like what?'

'Like this,' Jock said. He led the guardian to the door and, after fiddling with the mechanism once again, stood back and waited.

The guardian raised its arms and lunged heavily against the door, its metal paws striking the wood violently. At first nothing seemed to happen, but as the creature struck again the two friends heard the door groan and crack. With the next blow the wood around the bolt split apart and the door flung open.

'Aye, you're a good laddie,' Jock said, patting the creature's shoulder gently. A response seemed to glitter in the guardian's eyes, and as Jock stepped through the doorway, the creature followed him while Aramis shook his head with mild disbelief.

Ahead lay a dark corridor. They set off along this, the mechanical guardian padding noisily behind them.

The walls of the passage were damp and clammy to the touch and above their heads clumps of a strange stringy moss hung and dripped on them as they passed.

Jock checked on the guardian several times and, as he did, the creature lowered its head slightly to meet his gaze. 'That's a good lad,' Jock whispered. 'Come along.'

They followed the twists and turns of the passage as it wound deeper into the mountainside. After some time they heard the unmistakable sound of water echoing within some vast space. They moved ahead cautiously, attempting to make as little noise as possible. When they reached the end of the passage, they paused. Before them lay an extraordinary sight.

The passage opened onto a high walkway suspended within an enormous cavern that had been hollowed out within the interior of the mountain. Its dimensions were impossible to gauge—the arched roof soared above them until its contours were lost in total darkness.

Somewhere far below there flowed a slow moving river, the faint splashes resonating in hollow whispers around the massive space.

Jock and Aramis stepped onto the walkway, which ran around the perimeter of the cavern. It was fenced by light bronze railings, but these did little to provide any sense of security. Craning over the side, the two friends saw an immense drop beneath them.

About the vast chamber was a series of domes that had been constructed high above the ground, each on towering pillars of glistening rock that disappeared into the black waters below. Connecting the domes was a network of walkways.

Aramis pointed at the central dome, which was far bigger than the others. 'All the paths seem to converge *there*,' he said.

'Then odds on that's where we'll find the Baron,' said Jock.

'I'd say we have to pass through that smaller dome to reach the centre.'

Jock nodded and they headed onto one of the walkways. Small glimmering fragments of rock embedded into the sweeping walls gave the friends the impression that they were gliding among the stars.

Once across, they entered the dim structure. Deep, shadowy alcoves were recessed into its curved walls. A piece of the floor had fallen away, and through the wide gap came gusts of icy air, wafting up from the river far below. Jock and Aramis were surveying the room, when they were suddenly confronted by two brilliant green eyes. From one of the alcoves the ebony figure of Lady Nefertiti emerged from the shadows. She stopped in the centre of the room, her head tilted slightly as she studied the pair. An odd expression crossed her face as she noticed the guardian standing close behind Jock. 'Tell me,' she asked, 'how is it that you travel with the mechanical beast?'

Jock looked from the cat to the tall figure of the guardian and rested his paw on its cold arm. 'Never you mind,' he said. 'Where's your master?'

'I have no master,' she replied. 'And, as for the Baron, he is occupied.'

Aramis made a move, but she deftly raised a paw and flexed her sharp claws close to his face. 'And he does *not* want to be disturbed,' she said.

'No—not even by you, it would seem,' said Jock. 'Have you not wondered why he leaves you here alone while that gibbon accompanies him in his true work elsewhere?'

The cat turned her menace on him, her long claws still extended. 'And what do you know of the Baron's work?' she asked coldly.

'Enough to know that we must stop him.'

Nefertiti stood impassive, her long tail flicking slowly from side to side.

'Listen,' continued Jock, 'that Stone he carries—do you know what it is?'

She studied his face closely and slowly lowered her paw. '*What* it is?' she asked with interest.

'It is the prison containing the creature that ravaged this city *and* slew the race who built it.'

'*Creature?*' she said suspiciously.

'Aye, creature,' repeated Jock, 'or didn't the Baron share that detail with you? No,' he said dryly, 'I'm certain he did not. And I imagine there's plenty more he kept from your ears.'

As he stared into the cat's face he saw that he had judged rightly. While the gibbon and the Baron were drawn together by some peculiar bond, the cat was clearly the outsider—hired for her skills, but not privy to the Baron's secrets.

'How far,' said Jock keenly, 'are you really willing to trust this bear? What do you think he will do with the kind of power that can annihilate a race?'

Nefertiti studied the guardian and then Jock's face. Her voice was thinner than a whisper. 'Annihilate a race?' she said. She settled back on her hind legs, curling her long tail around her body so that its tip entwined about one of her front legs. 'And what do *you* propose?' she said, attempting to regain control.

'Well,' Jock said, as he stroked the guardian's plated arm. 'I might just have an idea. But at this point, it all really depends on you.'

Тhe воɾа

The large central dome of Kryl-Gavesk had once been magnificent. Suspended from the vaulted ceiling were three lights, pendulous tears of heavy glass supported by long spiralling arms of deeply burnished metal. Across the floor were the remains of several more of these lights; pieces of shattered crystal and bent metal scattered the length of the room. An immense circular table carved from a single piece of onyx lay upturned, as though some great hand had simply lifted it and flung it across the room. The walls were covered in scorch marks, and in places there were jagged rents in the stone itself. On the floor lay further skeletons, their gaunt limbs sprawled starkly across the cracked marble.

Standing beside one of these skeletons were the Baron and Philios Charon. In one paw the bear held the Binding Stone, and in the other a long staff. It was fashioned from many slender rods of silvery metal twisted tightly together. At the crown they flared out into a circle of small curving hooks, patiently awaiting the return of the Stone, which had been torn away from its setting so long ago.

With a look of great expectation in his dark eyes, the Baron gently set the Stone on top of the staff. It locked into place with a soft click that echoed dryly on the domed ceiling above.

'Baron,' a sweet voice purred from the other side of the room. The Baron and Philios turned and there, standing in one of the arched doorways, was Lady Nefertiti, her claws dug into the shoulder of Aramis Le Faye.

'Look what I found wandering about the corridors of Kryl-Gavesk,' she said, pushing Aramis forward.

The Baron drew his great paw across his muzzle and inspected Aramis closely. 'You seem determined to make an enemy of me,' he said finally. 'So, where is the other one?' he said to Lady Nefertiti.

'Ah, yes,' she replied delicately. 'I'm afraid I had to deal with him.'

The Baron raised an eyebrow. 'Indeed?'

The cat shrugged. 'The weasel was giving me lip—
I can't abide that,' she added, looking sideways at
Philios. 'You didn't *want* him alive, did you?'

A cold smile crossed the Baron's face. 'No,' he
murmured. 'Not exactly.' He stared down at Aramis
and his expression darkened. 'I told you it would go
poorly if I saw you again,' he said as he tightened his
paws around the staff. 'Do you think you are dealing
with a fool, Aramis Le Faye? Do you think I cast words
about idly? I told you when we first met that I was
unable to help you—you should have listened. But,
since you are so eager to know my business, I must not
disappoint you.'

Closing his eyes and drawing his brows tightly
together, the Baron began to chant in a sequence of
quivering musical syllables, like the song of a fast
moving stream. In response the mottled veins of black
and red within the Binding Stone grew more intense,
pulsing with a corrupt light. The Baron raised the staff
above his head, and the Stone then seemed to offer up
a song of its own, a strange and resentful howling.
Suddenly the symbols across its surface ignited, flaring
with a dark fire before abruptly fading away. And

there, standing in the centre of the vast chamber, was the Bora.

It stood more than twice as tall as the Baron, in form resembling a great bird. But it was more upright in posture than any bird and its body far bulkier. It appeared to be made of plates of jet black rock under which could be seen pulsing arteries of molten scarlet stone. All across its body, etched into the stony surface, were the imprints of thousands of tiny feathers. Wrapped about it were two vast wings, each ending in a grasping claw.

Its eyes were deep dark circles and set in the middle of each was a red pupil, like a beacon of fire burning on a dark plain. The only emotion in those eyes was an unending hatred.

After a moment the Bora opened its beaked mouth and spoke.

Its voice was unlike any sound Aramis had ever heard or imagined, so utterly hollow that it seemed to resonate from some distant past before the world was fashioned. If the black curtain on which the stars were woven had been given voice, it might have spoken thus.

'What is it that you bid me do?' the creature said, turning its malevolent eyes on the Baron.

'It is true, then?' The Baron breathed the words. 'I am the master.'

'It is true,' replied the Bora, its terrible voice ringing about the room. 'You hold the staff.'

'Then give me a small taste of what you can do,' said the Baron.

The Bora's talons gripped the marble flagstones and tore through them as though they were no more solid than sand. 'Does such a display please you?' it asked with contempt.

Without waiting for an answer, it stretched out a wing and laid its clawtip against the onyx table. The glassy stone exploded in a crown of crimson fire that left only a patch of black dust. 'Command me—but know that I hunger only for flame and ash,' the Bora said.

Beside the Baron, Philios Charon stared up at the great creature and his expression grew grim, his long fingers clenched into tight fists. Lady Nefertiti backed away towards the door, her normally serene face betraying her fear.

'So what now, Professor?' said Aramis. 'Now that you control this *thing,* what will you do?'

'What will I *do?* First I shall take my place as the rightful head of the Order of Symara. We will no longer study our art in the shadows, hiding like disgraced criminals. Sorcerers once ruled this continent—and they shall do so again.' As he scrutinised Aramis for a reaction, a wry half-smile drifted across his face. 'We will have a new Age of Magic—and I shall usher it in.'

'It appears that all my grandfather's instincts about you were right,' said Aramis.

'Watch what you say,' the Baron growled, his dark eyes lit with a dangerous flame. 'I command the Bora.'

'And so my grandfather could have done too,' said Aramis, 'but, unlike you, he did not hunger for power.'

'No,' the Baron returned swiftly. 'He merely feared it. Julius was craven. He would never have stood here— he lacked the true courage needed to pursue the Art. He was a fool—a failing which runs in the blood, I think.' The bear's voice swelled with anger. 'For who but a fool would dog my steps across the Wain, unarmed and unaided? And who but a fool would insult me where I stand—I who hold the unbound power of the Bora in my paws.'

He spun about to the great creature that stood unmoving in the centre of the room. Raising the staff, he said coldly, 'You are skilled in the arts of dealing death.' He pointed at Aramis. 'Show me—on him.'

The Bora acknowledged him. Aramis took a small step backwards, but suddenly a great compulsion came over him—a mastering desire to meet the creature's gaze, a desire that was not his own. Unwilling but unable to resist, he raised his eyes reluctantly to the Bora's.

'What's happening?' whispered Philios, drawing closer to the Baron.

'Quiet,' the bear said. 'Watch.'

Slowly, the expression on Aramis's face began to change. Into his mind there crept a series of images, like half-forgotten memories intruding on his consciousness. But they were not scenes from *his* past. He groaned and clamped his paws to his temples as a splinter of pain drove through the centre of his head. He began to perceive the monstrous place the Bora had been pulled from. He could see it unfold before him, at first as only a vision in his mind. But soon the Baron and Jock and Kryl-Gavesk and Bedlington and Merrin and all he had ever known fell away from him, and the other world was all he could see and hear—all he knew.

He stood under a cold red sun somewhere beyond the farthest star, before time and space. There was no place he could rest his mind. Everything his eyes passed across was terrifyingly alien. It was beyond nightmare;

beyond even madness. Upon vast plains other Bora tore through the blood-drenched earth, their kind in constant war with one another, with anything and everything. Above him, spilling from great rents in the sky, were flying ships filled with yet more Bora, along with worse beings, all shrieking in a hideous cacophony. He fell to his knees. Perhaps he cried out—he never knew.

And a great darkness descended on Aramis.

Jock hurried along one of the high walkways, his face grim. Close at his heels trod the mechanical guardian, the minute cogs in its chest whirring softly. As Jock went he thought over what Nefertiti had told him. If she was right about the other entrances to the main dome, then they still had a chance—as long as Aramis could keep the Baron distracted long enough. He swung round to see the guardian's perfect metallic face behind him.

They were halfway across when a low rumbling shook the cavern. To Jock's ears it sounded like thunder at first, but the noises slowly fashioned themselves into words. And into each word was poured a deep and violent hatred, a wretched abhorrence for all life. Swiftly after came the echo of some explosive fury— the rending and toppling of stone.

'Aramis!' gasped Jock. He raced to the far end of the walkway and swerved onto another path that led him through shadow to the far side of the great dome. Ahead he saw flashes of red light bursting from a doorway. Reaching the entrance he could see the Baron standing with his back to the door, the staff held high in his paws. Beside him was Philios Charon. Towering above all else in the room was the hideous form of the Bora, its face filled with a malevolent fire, its cruel beak held open as it stared at the far side of the room. Jock saw Aramis clutching his head in agony and watched in horror as his friend let out a tortured groan and collapsed heavily to his knees.

Jock quickly turned to the guardian, and his paws flew across its chest. 'Do not fail me, do not fail me,' he whispered urgently, as he furiously reset small dials in the creature's body. Across the room Nefertiti suddenly saw him, but betrayed no sign of his presence.

'Now!' hissed Jock, stepping aside. As he spoke the guardian lunged at the Baron, its full weight crashing into him from behind. The bear stumbled forward, the unexpected blow forcing him to his knees and knocking the staff from his paws. It rolled swiftly away from him and clattered across the marble floor, before coming to rest at Aramis's side.

As the staff left the Baron's paws, the Bora's beak closed and it stood motionless, its body pulsating with fluid streams of dark light.

'Aramis!' screamed Jock.

Aramis, still on his knees, weak and dazed, heard his friend's cry and felt the staff strike him. He stretched out his paws, grasped it with all his strength and drew it close to his body.

The Baron steadied himself and looked up to see Aramis holding the staff. Jock, Philios and Nefertiti watched in awe as Aramis and the Baron slowly rose to their feet, their eyes locking.

And in that instant of stillness the images of the Bora's world came again to Aramis's mind; the brutality and ceaseless death, the bitter craving for blood and chaos. The visions of that world seared his senses. A world of carnage and terror—but the only place where this creature belonged. There it had once dwelt before Elmasen magic had drawn it forth and imprisoned it. And to that place it had to be returned.

Glaring at the Bora, Aramis raised the staff steadily and in the eerie quiet of the room his voice rang out, the words clear and firm. 'I command you to return to your own realm,' he cried, 'to depart from this world forever.'

'No!' shouted the Baron in fury.

There was a flash of light, a trembling of the walls, then the Bora raised its head high and was consumed by darkness in a thunderous wail of sublime release. Where the great creature had stood there was now only a blackened shadow of scorched stone.

Aramis stared at the Baron, a grim expression upon his face. Slowly he turned the staff over in his paws and with sudden ferocity drove it into the ground at his feet, shattering the Binding Stone into hundreds of dull fragments.

Jock hurried across to where Aramis stood. As he tore through the room, the mechanical guardian fell in behind him once again.

'Easy, lad,' he said as he reached Aramis's side. He stretched out an arm to steady his friend, whose paws were still clasped weakly about the staff. 'It's all over now.'

'I think not,' stormed the Baron. He touched his neck and felt a trickle of blood on his paw where his clasp had cut him as he fell.

As he moved towards Jock and Aramis, the folds of his cloak rustled about him. His eyes were alight and across his face there passed an expression of black, unsatisfied hunger. Reaching under his cloak he grabbed his dagger and pulled it from its arm-brace with a flourish. He spoke a single graceful word and the red hilt began to shimmer and glow.

'This time,' he snarled, 'things will be done properly.' As Jock and Aramis edged backwards, the Baron raised his arm and flung the dagger across the room.

He had aimed not at them, however, but at the mechanical cat. It struck with tremendous force, the silver blade erupting with a sickly black flame as it lodged in the creature's exposed chest. The cat staggered feebly for a moment, then toppled backwards onto the marble floor with a deafening clang. It twitched briefly as the cogs in its ornate frame ground slowly into silence. As the fire of the knife blade waned so too did the warm light in the guardian's eyes, until they were no more than two pieces of cold garnet, forever dark.

Jock gasped and stretched out his paw towards the fallen guardian.

'Don't bother,' said the Baron dryly. 'That thing will not rise again.' Nefertiti was standing a little way behind them. 'Well, my Lady,' he said, 'your method of *dealing* with the weasel was somewhat lacking.'

'I knew she was rotten,' Philios hissed as he glared at the cat. 'I told you not to trust her.'

'You did indeed,' said the Baron. 'And she shall share the fate of those she aided.'

From one of his pouches he drew a vial of clouded glass. He crushed it swiftly in one of his great paws and as the thick liquid in it splashed across his claw tips, they ignited with cold fire.

'But first I think young Le Faye might sample a little of the Order's power,' he said softly. His face contorted into a fierce grimace and a burning trail of silver shot from his outstretched arm, arcing towards Aramis. But it did not strike him. As the energy exploded through the air a pale form appeared within the doorway and leapt forward. It landed before Jock and Aramis, its body shielding them from the light that spiralled from the Baron's upraised claws.

'Feldar!' cried Jock.

As he spoke, four more of the wolves slipped into the room, their red eyes piercing the dark.

'What are these things?' hissed Philios, drawing nearer the Baron.

'*These*,' said the Baron, 'would be the ghosts of the Wain. Do not let them trouble you,' he said and flung another stream of silver light towards Aramis. He watched as the wolf's body repulsed it.

'That magic cannot harm us,' said Feldar calmly.

'*No?*' said the Baron. 'Then let us see what can.' He lowered his paws and began to murmur. Around him a blue swirling haze gathered in a halo. A frenzied surge of power burnt through the air, showering Jock and Aramis with a fury of sparks. The wolves closed tightly around them to deflect the force back across the room. The whole dome shuddered, opening cracks in the thick floor and splintering the roof. The lights in the room trembled and rocked, the heavy arms of metal creaking and swaying.

The Baron glowered. At his feet a narrow fissure opened.

Philios gazed down apprehensively. '*Baron,*' he said in a tight whisper. But the bear did not hear. His face twisted, as though he sought to summon all the energy remaining to him and he hurled one final blast. It struck Feldar and ricocheted off the wolf, exploding about the walls and spraying rock and grit on all the animals.

The Baron stepped forward, his eyes ablaze, the crest at his throat splashed with blood.

'Baron!' Philios screamed as the ground beneath them roared and suddenly split apart. Philios gripped the Baron's cloak and together they fell, the bear's great paw grasping the edge of the shattered floor as they dangled above the abyss. He lunged with his other arm, but the weakened marble crumbled under his paw, and with a horrendous cry, he and Philios plunged into the dark crevasse.

For a moment afterwards all was still. Feldar bolted forward and stared down from the edge. He glanced up at the walls of the dome. 'We must leave,' he said. 'It is unsafe here.'

Aramis stood half-dazed, his fur matted with dust, the broken fragments of the Binding Stone scattered at his feet.

'Come on, Aramis,' said Jock softly, 'I'll give you a hand.' The figure of the guardian lay on the ground; its bejewelled eyes staring blindly. Stooping quickly, Jock removed the brass cylinder from the creature's frame and slipped it into his pocket. Then placing his arm firmly about Aramis's shoulder he began guiding him from the room.

Lady Nefertiti watched them leave and then padded to the edge of the crevasse. Stepping lightly on the scorched stone she craned her neck over the darkness, her ears twitching. She heard Jock's voice call, 'Get out of here, lass! It's not safe!'

'In my own time,' she whispered. She stood there poised for a moment. Then she left the dome.

Ahead she could make out the forms of Jock and Aramis as they followed the wolves in silence back along the walkway. She eyed the group hesitantly, then strode after them. She was only a few paces from the two friends when a deep rumble blasted the stillness. They turned and saw the great dome behind them begin to splinter and crumble and watched as it rocked briefly on its tall pillars before plunging into the depths. Tremors resounded through the cavern and clouds of dust spiralled towards them.

'Come!' cried Feldar.

And through the dead city of Kryl-Gavesk the Alessian wolves led the three animals. They tore breathless through its ancient halls and long passage-ways and came out at last into the stillness of the night.

CHAPTER FOURTEEN

The Return

A week had passed since their return and Jock and Aramis sat before the low fire, calm in the quiet of the evening. Stretching forward from his chair, Jock gave the logs a slow turn and watched as the embers flared and a stream of curling flames shot forth. Then he leant back and shut his eyes.

Aramis sat on the other side of the hearth, cradling a small cup. 'Winter will soon be upon us,' he said.

Jock nodded, his eyes still closed, the soft flickering of the fire throwing dappled patterns across his face. As he leaned further back in his deep chair, memories of all that had passed began edging once more into his thoughts.

He recalled the hollow sound of footfalls as they left the city and later the rise and fall of the land as they passed through the Wain by moonlight. Feldar had led them again over the Elmasen bridge, and with the Alessian flanking them on every side they had crossed its long span without incident.

A little way beyond this, Feldar had separated from the other wolves and continued as their sole guide, leading them around the marshes and to the eastern coast where their boat lay.

Parting from him on the clifftop, Jock had finally asked why he had come after them to the city—an act which had no doubt saved their lives. The wolf had answered softly, 'I had seen something in this world worth saving,' then had said no more as he padded away from them into the long night.

As Jock shifted in his chair, his eyes opened for a moment and caught the play of firelight upon the small cylinder of brass that now rested above the mantelpiece. He saw again the delicate face of the guardian and heard for a moment the steady whirring of its mechanical heart.

Jock sat up. The shifting hypnotic flames brought to mind the colours that had bathed the Tyresse Ocean at dawn. He saw the waters moving in the burnished spirals of flame, and closing his heavy eyes again, recalled their sombre voyage back to Bedlington, with Lady Nefertiti standing mutely at the prow, her large eyes turning from time to time to stare back to the bleak outline of the Wain.

He remembered how she had walked with them a little way through the docklands, and then when he turned to speak to her, found that she had vanished, her dark form lost amid the bustle of figures moving along the waterfront.

Jock rested his elbow on the arm of his chair and stroked his muzzle, wondering as he did so what had become of her.

Aramis was also reflecting on the recent events as if summoning a distant dream. He did not wish to dwell on their final moments in Kryl-Gavesk, and since their return had immersed himself in routine tasks, going about the town with Jock to buy some grain or to bargain for a sack of fresh vegetables.

He remembered that, after returning the *Manatee*, they had trudged wearily from the pier through the back lanes of Bedlington. Adeline had seen them as they had neared her shop, and with an unspoken understanding that something had befallen them, had ushered them inside. Though their clothes had been caked with grit and mud and their bodies were weary from travel, she had asked no prying questions. Sitting them down, she had given them hot drinks and laid out warm slices of bread. She had noticed the cut on Aramis's neck, prepared a poultice and handed it to him. 'For quick healing, sir,' she had told him in her soft, reassuring voice.

As they had left, she lingered for a moment on her doorstep watching them. 'Take care of yourself, sir,' she had called. 'And you too, Mr Jock,' she had added gently.

Aramis raised his paw and drew it idly across the small scar on his neck. Jock had insisted he stay on for a while, and even though Aramis's thoughts often turned to his small house back in Merrin, he found that he had grown to love the sights and sounds of Bedlington; the call of gulls high on the salty air and the bustling activity of the markets.

On their second day back in town he had gone with Jock to Milton's and told him all that had happened. Milton had listened to every word of their story and looked at them in astonishment when told about the breaking of the Stone. At the news of the Baron's fall he had nodded slowly. 'And yet you survived,' he had said quietly, his eyes resting on Aramis, 'and put your grandfather's fears forever to rest.'

Aramis sighed and leaned further back into the chair, listening to the clock tick softly in the hallway and the light rain rap against the window and splash in the cobbled streets.

'Well, lad,' said Jock softly, his voice edging into his friend's reveries. 'It's probably time I turned in.' He rose slowly from his chair and shuffled towards the hallway. 'Goodnight, Aramis,' he called.

'Goodnight, Jock,' Aramis breathed deeply, as he stared into the dancing flames.

Far from the hearth and a waiting bed, however, something was stirring. Under the faint moonlight, two weary figures emerged from the shadowy chambers of Kryl-Gavesk. The claws of the Baron were deeply scratched and grimed with filth and mud, but he had survived and now stood defiantly on the valley floor, his great chest heaving, his eyes raised to the stars.

Philios Charon was slumped at his side, dazed and gaunt with hunger—his throat too dry to break the silence that hung heavily over them. He shivered as the chill breath of the night air swept through the courtyard, and stumbled as he began to move again.

The Baron's arm quickly caught and steadied him. 'Come, Philios,' he said, 'and we shall leave this place.'

Turning back one last time to gaze at the city, the two continued their journey into the dark.

Ewan Battersby was born in Australia and lives in Sydney. His interests include music and film. *Jock and Aramis* is Ewan's first novel.

Dianne Speter attended art school before completing a degree in English literature. Her interests include animals, painting, plants and science fiction films. *Jock and Aramis* is her first novel.